PRAISE FOR JACQUIE BIGGAR

Crazy Little Thing Called Love

A touching, heartwarming story that takes your breath away.

Characters that will have you feeling so many emotions. It deals with family, misunderstandings, ranch life, horses, life long love and of course Pumpkin the cat.

Tony and Sophia's story had me laughing, crying and a bit frustrated with them at times. To me that is good writing when I can be moved to so many emotions while reading . The story is so good, I couldn't put it down.

— B

With This Heart

Such a sweet heartwarming romance about second chance love between two people who are obviously meant to be together. You won't want to put this story down until you're finished reading.

This is a wonderful series. Those of you who love military romance, wounded warrior romance and romantic suspense will love the stories written by this super talented, fabulous author!

— TAMMY

Maggie's Revenge

The first comment I can easily make here is: MAGGIE'S REVENGE punched my 'WOW' button!

Magdalena Holt goes rogue and deep undercover for the DEA... Fast forward: > Olga, a once teenage prostitute, and four others are captured by 'sex traffickers', put in a 'mud pit' basement. After several attempts, beatings, torture, and a lot of action, the group of five make their escape...

The suspense is staggering as 'Maggie' and her tattered and broken group valiantly withstand the vagaries of the Mexican compound and hell-hole, escape, and then await the DEA to recover them. Maggie wants to get home and bring down the most evil man she has ever known...a criminal and terrifying clown named Chenglei.

The romantic component in this exciting novel involves Maggie's partner and agency member, Adam O'Connor, who the boss fears will jeopardize rescue efforts because he is 'too close' - with his feelings for Maggie.

MAGGIE'S REVENGE is masterfully written and a 'must read' for the 'mystery and suspense' book lovers! The novel would also make a great movie! It's been a while since I've seen this 'theme' in movies...of course, I only watch an occasional TV movie.

— JULIE GEHRANDT

SWEETHEART COVE

BLUE HAVEN- BOOK 1

JACQUIE BIGGAR

WAVEFRONT PUBLISHING

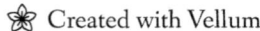

For my Family
If not for your encouragement, I may never have strived
to become a writer.
Now, I can't imagine any occupation that could better
allow me to live my dreams.

Love ya always and all ways,
Jacq

If you find someone you love in your life, then hang on to that love.

— PRINCESS DIANA

INTRODUCTION

Josie wasn't sure how she got through the next few days. She must have acted reasonably normal because no one questioned her absentmindedness, even when she set the puppy's food in the refrigerator instead of the pantry where it belonged. Jacob's kiss lived front and center in her thoughts, and his hard, masculine body encompassed her dreams. A moody, short-tempered grump who made her pulse skyrocket.

How could she feel this way about him when she'd been hours from marrying another man a month ago? She added fresh-baked chocolate chip cookies to the picnic basket she'd prepared and glanced down at the pup sitting quietly at her feet. "If you're looking for handouts, you'll just have to wait. No offence, but I don't trust your stomach in the car."

"Is it time yet?" Jane wheeled into the kitchen, her

face expectant. The dog, thinking it was playtime, crouched, nose on his front paws, butt in the air and tail wagging a mile a minute. He let out a couple of excited yips, then raced around the room and jumped against Jane's short-clad legs. "Ow, Mischief, that hurts," she cried, then stopped in shock and stared at the red marks already fading from her skin. "It hurt," she whispered.

Josie pushed the dog out of the way and crouched at the little girl's side. "Honey, this is great. I'm so happy for you. We better tell your father, so he can get you into the specialist for a checkup."

Jane shook her head and gripped Josie's wrist. "No. Can we keep it a secret? Please, Josie? Just for a while. I want to get better and surprise Daddy by walking. *Please?*"

Her pleading eyes undid Josie. How was she supposed to say no to that? She nodded. "Okay, but if you have any pains at all, you tell me, understand?" She patted Mischief's silky head. "Guess your dad knew what he was doing, getting you a dog. Maybe we should name him Miracle instead of Mischief."

Jane giggled. "It's not Mischief, Josie. It's you. You're the miracle."

JACQUIE BIGGAR

SWEETHEART COVE

BLUE
HAVEN
#1

The clouds briefly parted beneath the seaplane, affording Josie her first glimpse of the Pacific Northwest island that would be her new home for the summer—Sweetheart Cove. Blue Haven Island was small and loosely shaped like a heart. The town sat nestled in the bosom of two mountainous ridges. Not quite the Caribbean getaway she should have been enjoying with her new husband—the rat fink.

She caught herself rubbing the faint indentation on her ring finger with her thumb and stopped. He'd done her a favor. Better she learned the kind of man he was now, before there were children involved. She'd been there, it was no fun being used as a bargaining chip in your parents' divorce proceedings.

The plane hit a pocket of turbulence and she gasped, her stomach sky-diving down to her toes. She clenched the arms of the seat and closed her eyes, a silent plea rolling off her lips. It would figure if her first experience on an airplane included a crash.

"You can quit praying now, we're there," an amused voice said.

Josie blinked and looked across the center row at the only other passenger on this flight. *Rugged.* That had been her first impression upon boarding, quickly followed by big, broad, mesmerizing. His dark hair glinted under the recessed lighting, wavy and overlong, curling against the collar of his shirt. Laughter lines gave character to the silvery, blue-gray eyes staring at her with blatant male interest. Long, muscular legs covered in well-worn jeans filled the space between the seats giving the impression of height and strength.

"Cat got your tongue?" he asked, holding out a lean, tanned hand.

Josie blushed and thrust her fingers into his. "Josie Sparks. I'm not a frequent flyer, as you may have already guessed."

"I wouldn't worry, Troy's been doing this run for a lot of years, he won't let anything happen to his favorite girl." She stared at him, confused and he grinned. He nodded out the window. "The plane; he named her after his daughter, The Betsy Boop."

She smiled nervously, tugging to get her hand back. "I'll take your word for it, Mr....?"

He gave it a little squeeze before letting go with seeming reluctance. Josie's pulse spiraled. "Samuels. Jacob Samuels. I run the lumber yard and hire out for home construction in my spare time. What brings you to our little piece of Pacific paradise, Josie Sparks?"

Whoa. The way he looked at her as he said her name created more than sparks, how about a raging wildfire? Time to back away before she got burnt.

She held up her left hand and wriggled her fingers, making sure he noticed the pale band on her skin where her engagement ring had been. "You've heard of the runaway bride? Well, in my case it's the groom." His brows lowered, and she waved away the questions she could see forming. "Suffice to say, I've learned my lesson. Anyway, I needed to escape the sympathetic eyes of our friends and family, so I looked online for a summer job and came across a caregiver position for a six-year-old girl, room and board included. And, here I am." *Lost and pathetic*, but she didn't add those words. She'd already said enough to scare him off. He'd changed position as she talked, angling away from her, his profile losing its warmth, turning aloof as he stared out the window. "Umm, did I say something wrong?"

His mouth lowered at the corners, his lips little more than an angry slash. "You're supposed to be old," he snapped.

She sat back, stunned. Talk about your hot to cold

emotions. Good thing she wasn't interested in an affair, this guy was nuts.

"Pardon me?" she asked, not sure she'd heard him correctly.

He seared her with those gunmetal eyes. "*I* hired the nanny, Miss Sparks. But she sure isn't supposed to look like you."

Josie shook her head. The universe had it out for her, that's all there was to it. "So, you're my new boss?"

He crossed his arms and stared down the bridge of his slightly crooked nose. Probably received in a street brawl, she figured.

"Until I find a way to cancel your contract," he agreed.

Josie sighed. Maybe the plane would crash and put her out of her misery.

J ake couldn't wait to get off the plane and talk to Mona. His sister had better have a damn good explanation for going against his demands. He wouldn't put it past her to have picked Josie off one of those dating sites! He'd specifically told her he was looking for a grandmotherly woman to take care of Jane over the summer break. If Josie Sparks was a senior, he'd eat his hat. He glanced her way, taking in the wavy brown hair bunched into a thick ponytail, the white t-shirt with the words *life's a beach,* written across her generous breasts—not that he was looking—and pink toenails peeking from under the hem of her linen pants. She didn't seem much older than his niece, Samantha, who'd promised to take care of Jane at the café until she'd gone and broken her leg skateboarding last week. Mona had insisted placing an ad online would be the fastest way to fill the position, so he'd agreed—with the provision she chose a responsible person for the position. He had a crazy schedule this summer and couldn't afford to be worrying whether Jane had adequate supervision. He'd argued with her about it before he'd left on his business trip.

"Don't be such a worry wart, brother of mine. You know I'd be more than happy to keep Janie with me, but she'd be bored silly sitting around the restaurant day after day. It wasn't so bad when Sam was going to watch her, she could have kept her busy, but now..." Mona had shrugged and continued tallying up the cash register after the day's sales. "Business has picked up since that new health spa broke ground by the beach. Good thing the town was able to convince that creep, Trace Michaels, to allow it into the cove."

Jake shook his head, well aware of his sister's animosity to the mayor of Sweetheart Cove. "Trace was rightfully worried about damage to the shoreline. Why don't you cut him a break? It's been sixteen years since he stood you up for the prom. Time to get over it, sis."

Her expression resembled the thunderclouds that had been hovering over the island for the past week. "It's got nothing to do with high school, Jake. What do you take me for?" She slammed the till shut with a clang. "As a member of the tourism board, it's my duty to investigate all viable options to bring travelers to town and thereby create some much-needed income for the region. Trace bucks every idea I have. If it were up to him we'd still be in the nineteenth century, I'm sure. Why you always defend him, I'll never understand."

She'd stomped into the kitchen, the swinging doors banging behind her ramrod stiff back, leaving Jake to wonder how the conversation had disintegrated into a mud-slinging match.

He stared at the beautiful troublemaker squeezing the life out of the armrests as the plane made its descent. "Where are you staying, Miss Sparks?" he asked, not really caring but hoping to take her mind off the landing which could be a bit choppy depending on the wind.

She opened large green deer-in-the-headlights eyes and licked her lips. "Wha...what?"

He was temporarily distracted by that pink tongue. "I, ah... I said where are you planning to stay while you visit the island?"

"Umm, I was promised a room next to the little girl's, so I could be near if she needed me."

Of course.

"I'll put you up at a hotel until you can make arrangements to return to the mainland. At my expense," he hurried to add. It wasn't her fault his sister was an idiot.

"Look, I'm already here. Why not give me a chance?" she said, her voice squeaky as the ocean rushed up to meet the pontoons. The plane touched down with barely a bump, carrying them effortlessly toward the harbor.

"You do realize my daughter and I live alone, Miss Sparks? It wouldn't be right." God, could he sound more prudish?

The plane idled down and stopped, leaving the water gently clapping against the side of the dock. He'd been born and raised on this island, it was in his blood. He'd grown up hiking forest trails half-hidden by giant ferns, kayaking with orcas and seals, snorkeling the reefs with octopus and salmon, and biking hills that rose to meet the clouds. Activities he'd looked forward to sharing with his beautiful wife, Annie, and their perfect baby daughter.

Until the accident.

"I don't sleepwalk, Mr. Samuels. Your virtue is perfectly safe with me." Josie unclipped her seatbelt and rose, bestowing a warm smile on Troy who'd opened the door and now stood waiting to help them exit, his lips quirking at their little exchange.

Jacob shot him a tell-anyone-and-you're-dead glare, hurrying to follow the annoying woman off the plane.

"Not a word," he muttered, brushing by a now openly smiling Troy.

"See you next week," the pilot said, raising an acknowledging hand before unloading a couple of bulging suitcases, climbing aboard and shutting the door. Two-point-five seconds later, Troy was lifting off and he and Josie were left awkwardly staring at each other.

Josie dropped her gaze first, reaching for the pull handles on her bags. "Okay, well, I wish I could say it's been a pleasure, but..." She yanked the bags down the wharf, her heels catching in the grooves between the boards.

Jacob tipped his head back and stared at the azure sky. She wasn't his problem. He had more than enough to worry about. She'd find her way to the hotel, spend a few days touring the island, then go back to wherever it was she'd come from. Case closed.

"Miss Sparks," he called, heaving a world-weary sigh. She was industrious, he'd give her that. She'd already left the dock and started the climb to town, her suitcases bumping clumsily up each stair. "Miss Sparks, wait." He strode after her, the briny scent of the sea for once not doing anything to calm his mood.

"I think you've made your point," she said, her voice breathless as she scowled at him.

That tone sent goosebumps stumbling over each

other down his spine. Shit, this was such a bad idea. "Okay, you win. I need a sitter and you need a place to stay. We'll try it out for a week—if it isn't working you go home with Troy on his next trip, agreed?"

She rested a hand on a slim hip and took her sweet time giving him an answer. Just when he was ready to say forget it, she smiled.

"Agreed."

3

The house sat on a cliff overlooking Sweetheart Cove and the bay beyond. It was a sprawling ranch-style home bordered by an acre of park-like grounds. Josie didn't know much about architecture but couldn't fail to notice the cream stucco façade and dark roof blended into its surroundings as though it had always been there. One wall seemed entirely made up of tinted glass that reflected the gently swaying cedars and the plume of a jet high overhead. The asphalt drive took them to a three-car garage with a mean-looking black motorcycle parked off to one side. It reminded her of the grim man who'd driven them up here. His truck was older, but clean, the back filled with an assortment of lumber.

"You have a lovely home," she ventured, peeking at him from the corner of her eye.

If anything, his expression turned darker. "Let's get this over with, I have business to attend to this afternoon." He opened his door and hopped out, slamming it on his way to grabbing her bags from the back.

Alrighty then.

She was beginning to wonder if the pay she'd been offered was worth putting up with Mr. Tall, Dark, and Incredibly Ornery. The woman who'd hired Josie over the phone—his sister—assured her she'd have very little to do with the father, it was the little girl who needed her care. Apparently, she'd lost her mother in a car accident a couple of years ago and been seriously injured herself. Josie's soft heart filled with empathy. How horrible to witness the death of a parent at any age, never mind as a young child. She didn't know if she'd be able to help this troubled family, but she had to try.

By the time she exited the vehicle, Jacob had her suitcases—one in each hand—and was waiting impatiently for her to join him on the flagstone sidewalk leading around to the impressive front door. She gave him an impudent lift of the chin, refusing to allow his negativity to intimidate her. She'd dealt with domineering men before and found the more you give in to them, the worse it gets.

"This way, Miss Sparks." He stepped aside for her to lead the way, and she fancied she could feel his hot breath on her nape. She shivered, her heart giving a funny little flip in her breast.

Then the door opened, and she forgot the man. The most exquisitely beautiful girl wheeled out of the house in an electric wheelchair, a harassed-looking woman following close behind.

"I told her to wait and you'd be right in, but..."

"It's fine, she's probably anxious to meet our *guest*." Jacob's voice startled Josie with its warmth. She glanced over her shoulder and caught a heart-stopping smile aimed at his daughter. It slipped when he noticed her looking at him, and his quicksilver eyes sent her a warning glare. What did he think she was going to do to the poor kid?

Josie met the woman's sympathetic gaze—the sister, going by the strong family resemblance—before crouching beside the wheelchair and solemnly holding out her hand. "Hi, I'm Josie. I'm new to the island and could use someone to show me around. Interested?"

Golden-brown almond shaped eyes stared at her curiously, a hint of loneliness flirting in the shadows of her expression. "I don't like cars," she said.

"Jane," her father beseeched. "You need to get past this, pumpkin. You don't want to be stuck here with your doddering old dad when you grow up, do you?"

There wasn't anyone less doddering than Jacob Samuels.

The color leeched from Jane's cheeks, her fingers tiny talons digging into Josie's palm. "Don't you want me anymore, Daddy?"

The sister gasped. "Jane, you know that's not true!"

There was a thunk as her suitcases hit the sidewalk and Jacob joined her on the opposite side of the wheelchair, his arms reaching to pull his child close— breaking her grip on Josie's hand. She rubbed it absently, touched by the obvious connection between father and daughter. He might have a core of steel, but it turned to putty under liquid brown eyes.

"As you probably already guessed, I'm Mona, Jake's sister. It's a pleasure to finally meet you." Mona smiled and patted her brother's shoulder. "Let's leave these two to bring in your luggage, I'll show you around the house."

Josie rose, but hesitated, gazing at her soon-to-be charge. "Maybe I should..."

Jacob looked up, Jane's face buried against his neck, his hand cradling her curly brown hair. "Don't worry, Miss Sparks. My daughter is perfectly safe with me."

Heat flooded her cheeks. "I never thought any different."

She followed Mona into the sanctuary of the house, away from the condemning gaze of her host. The rooms were large and airy, floors covered in hardwood and the furniture spaced to allow easy wheelchair access. She was relieved to see the master bedroom on the opposite end of the house. An expansive kitchen filled with state-of-the-art equipment and an over-sized island complete with bar stools opened into a living room right out of a magazine. Floor-to-ceiling windows took up the far wall, giving a birds-eye view of the bay far below. A gorgeous stone fireplace flanked by a dark leather sofa and two plush club chairs promised warm, cozy, intimate nights.

And *why* was she thinking those sorts of thoughts?

Down a short hall a large, spa-like bathroom combined with a walk-in shower large enough for two separated her and Jane's rooms.

"Jane does well on her own, but Jake prefers someone to be close just in case." Mona gestured around the spacious bedroom. "Well, what do you think? Can you put up with my overbearing brother for a couple of months?"

Josie eyed the four-poster bed and nodded. Having a roof over her head trumped Mr. Grumpy Pants. Besides, according to Mona's earlier phone call, he was a busy man and wouldn't be around the house much. She pushed aside the memory of him hugging his daughter. "I'm sure we'll be fine. Your niece seems like a real sweetheart." She hesitated. "Is there any chance...?"

Mona strode to the window and looked out. "That she'll walk again?" She turned and faced Josie. "The doctors don't know. There was a lot of nerve damage, and the trauma... Let's just say, they don't hold out much hope." She retraced her steps to the door. "I'll let you get settled now. I promised Jake I'd stay until after lunch, so take your time. Peanut and I are going to bake some cookies." She smiled and left the room, closing the door gently behind her.

Josie stood in the middle of the room, her stomach sinking. How was she supposed to keep a happy-go-lucky visage up with a broken little angel and a man who evoked tender feelings even as he shoved everyone away?

4

Jake sat at the kitchen counter, enjoying the rare joy on his daughter's face as she helped Mona decorate the freshly baked cookies with sparkles and colorful icing. Jane finished the one she'd been working on, a fair imitation of a cat with rainbow whiskers, and held it up for her dad to see.

"What do you think, Daddy? Aunty said if I keep practicing I can sell some at the county fair. She said it's tons of fun. They have games, and rides, and even a petting zoo. Can we go, Daddy? Can we?"

He met Mona's faux innocent look over Jane's head before turning his attention to his girl. "The fair is a long way from here. The only way to get there would be by car, sweetheart." His gut twisted at her crestfallen expression. "I think your cookies look delicious.

How about you sell them to me and I'll take them to work? The guys will love them."

Jane set the cookie on the platter, avoiding his gaze. "Sure, whatever." She pushed the wheelchair away from her work counter, specially made for her height. "I'm tired. I'm going to lay down for a while. Thanks, Aunty Mona, I had fun."

Mona waved a piping bag in the air. "Next time we'll try cupcakes. Sweet dreams, honeybun."

Jake waited until the whir from Jane's wheelchair faded away before confronting his sister. "Why do you keep making promises you know you can't keep?" He pushed the offending cookie platter aside and glared at the smear of purple icing on his palm.

Mona handed him a damp dish cloth without a word, then turned to pull the last pan out of the oven. The tempting aroma of peanut butter filled the air. She scooped the cookies onto the waiting sheet of waxed paper, set the pot holders on the counter and loaded the sink with the dirty dishes.

Jake swiped ineffectually at his hand and frowned. "Aren't we a little old for the silent treatment?" He'd hated it as a child and didn't care for it much now, either.

She turned off the taps and swung around to face him, hands fisted on her hips. "You coddle that child too much, Jacob. You aren't doing her any favors. The doctor told us it'll only get harder to bring her out of her shell as time passes. You're making her into a recluse."

He stiffened. She had no right... He was only protecting the one thing he had left in this world. Who could blame Jane for not wanting to get into a car again? She'd lost her mother, for crying-out-loud!

"The *doctor* wasn't there," he snapped. "She'll do things in her own time. I won't allow anyone to rush her into something she's not ready for. That'll do more harm than letting her stay home where she feels safe."

Mona sighed and handed him a dish towel. "Come help me with these." She took the proffered cloth and started to wash the soaking pans. "I guess I owe you an apology." She kept her head down and tried to scrub the pattern off the dessert plate. "I'm only trying to help."

Jake dunked his hand in the water—did she need it set to scalding?—and stopped her frantic scouring. "I know you are, but you need to give Jane time. She's still getting used to the changes in her life. The counselor assures me the panic attacks will pass when she's ready. Our job is to love and support her."

"When I think of the jerk who did this...," Mona whispered, her gaze moist.

He couldn't go there. It would suck him into the empty well of his soul if he did. He gave her hand a comforting squeeze, before picking up a bowl to dry. "Tell me about our new therapist. Did you check her credentials? She's young." *Too young.*

Mona slanted him a glance while handing over a cleaned cookie sheet. "She comes highly recommended, Jake. I wouldn't hire just anyone, you know. She's a physiatrist and knows what she's doing."

"Then why isn't she working in a hospital somewhere?" he retorted. He wasn't usually so judgmental, but this was his daughter, and something about Josie Sparks bothered him.

"I was, up until my fiancé, who just happened to be the head of our department, dumped me for my maid-of-honor on the eve of our wedding."

He swore under his breath and shot a thanks-for-the-warning glare at his sister before turning to face his uninvited guest. "I'm sorry that happened to you," he said, and meant it. Guys who screwed around were pond scum in his book. "But you have to understand why I'm concerned. I was expecting someone more..."

"Mature?" she suggested, her gaze knowing. "Rest assured, Mr. Samuels, I'm good at my job. Your daughter will be safe with me. I gave your sister references, if that helps."

"That's not necessary, the hospital was quite sorry to see you go," Mona piped up. "Jacob just likes to worry, don't you, Jake?"

He crossed his arms over his chest and looked down his nose at the newcomer. "I think that's a father's prerogative. I'll take those references, if you don't mind, Miss Sparks?"

"Jake," his sister hissed. "Don't be rude."

Josie smiled, though he could see he'd upset her. Well, too bad. He wasn't out to make friends, and especially not with a green-eyed minx.

"No, it's all right. I understand. You're just protecting your child," she said. "I'll wait to start until you've had a chance to make the calls. Tomorrow morning, okay?"

He slowly nodded, aware that she hadn't given up. "Tomorrow is fine. But, I want a complete list of your planned treatment, and it must be cleared by me before you implement anything new. Understood?"

She gave him a sharp nod and smiled reassuringly at his sister. "Completely. Now, if you don't mind, I'm going to unpack and have a look around—since I have a day off."

Mona snickered. "That's it, hon. Don't let him intimidate you, his bark is worse than his bite."

Jake had the urge to show his teeth, there was no denying that.

5

Josie wandered down the country road leading into town. She admired the giant ferns and moss-covered rocks lining the ditches like something out of a Jurassic movie. Bluebells and wild geraniums provided splashes of color and ivy clung to the massive trunks of hemlock and cedar. The cheerful songs of birds in the trees accompanied her steps. Maybe she'd have time to take up birdwatching while she was on the island. Though if her new boss wasn't going to let her do her job she wouldn't be around long enough to take up the hobby. She could see glimpses of the Pacific Ocean through the trees, teasing her with its poignant beauty—and reminding her of Jacob's eyes.

Mona had briefly explained the circumstances surrounding her niece's condition during the phone interview. A drunk driver had driven through a stop sign and broadsided the Samuels' vehicle, instantly killing Jake's wife and gravely injuring his four-year-old daughter. It was obvious the family was still going through the grieving process and Josie's heart went out to the little girl who'd lost her mother. Josie's feelings for the father were far more complicated.

A path opened up on the right leading toward the water and she decided to take it. Good thing she'd worn sturdy shoes. While the descent was gradual, the gravel could have proven treacherous without proper footwear. The sounds of distant traffic from the road faded, covered by sighing trees and the slap of waves hitting the rocks below. The trail widened onto a beach littered with driftwood like hulking gray corpses. She looked up and down the stretch of sand, maybe a kilometer long, but there was no one in sight except for the swooping, gliding seagulls searching for their next meal. A couple of sailboats floated out in the water, their owners enjoying the near-perfect conditions.

Josie sighed and sank onto the sand. Emmett would have loved this place. It'd been his dream to go to an island for their honeymoon—though he'd chosen the Bahamas. How could she not have seen what was going on right beneath her nose? It was the humiliation that was getting to her, which told her something right there —if she was listening. Maybe, it was more about the getting married than the man, in which case she'd dodged a bullet. Emmett was better off with Nurse Skanky-Pants, though it rankled she was going to get to enjoy the five-star resort Josie had searched months to find. Her mother hadn't understood why she couldn't forgive and forget, after all, *she was lucky Emmett chose her*. Like she was a piece of furniture or something. Josie loved her parents, but their archaic morals tended to drive her crazy. It was bad enough she had to make the dreaded phone calls to family and friends warning them not to make an as-it-turned-out unnecessary trip for the wedding, she'd also endured a twenty-five minute lecture on how to be a good wife! Apparently, men were excused their immoral behavior as long as they kept the home fires burning. It shed a new and disturbing light on some of her father's supposed business trips, one she decided not to dwell on.

A harbour seal poked its sleek gray head out of the water, a fish struggling to escape its whiskered mouth. Before Josie had time to feel sorry for the fish, a Bald Eagle swept out of the sky and snatched the easy meal. Stunned, she stared at the hapless seal until it disappeared under the waves, hungry and no doubt disappointed. She knew just how the poor guy felt. Not that she'd actually had her teeth into her fiancé, but he'd definitely been stolen by an unexpected predator. Simone was supposed to be her best friend, her bridesmaid. She'd lost two of the most important people in her life thanks to the betrayal. Now she had to figure out how to move on from here. There was no way she was going back to the hospital where they had worked together, that's for sure.

"What do you think of our island?"

Josie jumped, startled by the male voice coming from over her shoulder. Her pulse skipped, and she knew without looking who had come to destroy her peaceful sanctuary—Jacob.

JAKE STARED down at the young woman who had disturbed his home and wondered why he'd followed her down to the beach. He should have been heading up-island to the construction site. He was already running close to the deadline and couldn't afford any more lost days, yet here he was.

She tipped her head to meet his gaze, honey-brown hair cascading down her slim back. "What I've seen so far is beautiful. I can understand why you love it here. It's a charming place to raise a family." Her eyes grew wide and she covered her mouth, then slowly lowered her hand. "I'm sorry, I didn't mean to bring up painful memories."

Jake ignored the pinch of his heart and nodded to the spot next to her. "Mind if I join you?" He needed to talk where there was no fear of being overheard. There were issues with Jane the therapist should know about; things that worried him sick.

"Not at all." She scooted over and made room, careful to keep her legs slanted away from his as he sat on the warm sand. She glanced at him from under her sun-kissed lashes, her smile wary. "Did you change your mind and decide to let me go after all?"

He picked up a shell and turned it over in his hand, admiring the strength to survive stormy seas even though he could crush it beneath his foot. He handed the pretty piece over. "My daughter means the world to me, Miss Sparks. She's gone through a traumatic time and is only just starting her recovery period. If... and I stress *if*, you're going to be her caregiver there are things you should know."

Josie presented her profile to him as she stared out at the sparkling water. "You don't have to tell me about your wife, if that's what you mean." She turned to him, empathy making her eyes a luminous blue-green. "I'm very sorry for your loss, but I truly believe I can help Jane with her mobility issues. I also have a degree in psychology. Sometimes, an impartial ear can make a difference. Please...," she placed a hand on his bent knee, "give me a chance."

Jake was filled with conflicting emotions. He had to physically restrain himself from reaching out to grasp those slim fingers with their pretty pink polish and either hang on or fling it away. Why was he attracted to her? The feeling felt foreign, wrong. He'd met and married Annie right out of high school. They'd been together eight years before Jane was born. Annie had been to countless fertility specialists on the mainland and endured monthly exams while she took the dangerous drugs to strengthen the walls of her uterus. He'd tried to convince her to consider adoption, but her heart was set on giving birth. Sex became more of a by-appointment affair, depending on her temperature readings and the optimal time for fertilization.

But then Jane came along, and life was good.

Until it wasn't.

He stood, ignoring the loss her touch left, and pursed his lips. "You've got your chance, Josie. Don't make me sorry I agreed."

She rose at his side, her diminutive figure raising more urges he refused to feel.

"Can I bring her here, to the beach one day?" She pointed toward the water. "There are studies on the benefits of salt water as a muscular therapy. I would like to try it out with Jane, just a few minutes at a time until we see if it's helping." She smiled up at him, encouraging him to have faith. "I can print the research off first, if you'd like. It has shown positive results in almost eighty percent of test subjects."

Jake stiffened, his old friend anger returning in a red-hot flash. "My daughter is *not* a test subject. Miss Sparks. If that's the reason you're here, you may as well pack your bags now." He should have known. She was way to... pretty to stick herself on a small island watching after a child. There was always a catch.

"Do you ever plan on getting over that inflated ego you're carting around? I've said adnauseum why I'm here. If that's not good enough for you, then fine. I'll leave today." Josie's friendly smile disappeared into a cloudburst every bit as volatile as his own. If he wasn't so angry, he might have been a little turned on. Just a little, mind you.

She stomped up the incline away from the beach, her feet sending little tufts of dust flying into the air. Suddenly, Jake had the urge to smile.

"Miss Sparks," he called.

She slowed to a halt and swung to face him, hands fisted on her hips and chest heaving from exertion. A pint-sized Amazon warrior princess.

"I apologize. Please stay." He was surprised by how important her answer was.

She hesitated, then gave one short nod before carrying on up the path.

Jake sighed. This was going to be an interesting summer.

6

Mona reached into the glass-fronted counter and withdrew a thick slice of homemade blackberry pie. She made a mental note to come into work early tomorrow, so she could make more desserts before the restaurant opened. It had taken time to get the hang of baking after Annie died—she'd been the baker while Mona handled the cooking—but the customers had rallied behind her efforts, thank goodness. Being a single parent meant she had all of the financial worries as well as raising her daughter. Showing up at sports tournaments and volunteering at the school fell to her overloaded shoulders. When her sister-in-law was alive, she'd taken up some of the slack, happy to care for her young niece while Jacob was at work.

Mona moved to the ice cream counter, slid the

heavy glass door open and added two heaping scoops of French vanilla to the pie. It looked like a snowman on steroids. "Here you go, Mr. Hayward. Just the way you like it." She smiled and set the plate in front of the senior.

"Perfect end to a perfect meal, Mona." He picked up his fork, the tremble in his fingers making it ring against the plate. "Ain't no wonder my Sally wants to put me on a diet."

Mona patted his liver-spotted hand resting on the table. "You tell Sally to come see me, I'll set her straight. You're skin and bones as it is."

He cackled and got down to the business of polishing off his dinner, his mind eased by her response. Really, that Sally Michaels should know better. Her father had been coming to the diner for ten years or more and hadn't gained an ounce that Mona could see. Sally was just bitter because her papa preferred Mona's cooking over her own. Kind of like her husband had once desired Mona. It'd been before they were married, but still, Sally had never gotten over it. Then again, neither had she.

The rise and fall of voices blended with the country music piped in through overhead speakers. The island was too small to support more than one radio station and the owner, Burt Cummings, didn't believe in that 'new age crap' as he called it. Mona didn't mind, at least she could understand the words, even if most of the songs were about lost love. She'd made peace with her past long ago.

"Daddy, there you are." Speak of the devil. Sally wound her svelte body between the tables, an oversized black designer handbag hanging from a silk-clad shoulder. Chandelier earrings mesmerized the eye, swinging like pendulums with every stride. A perfect complexion highlighted the sophisticated twist she'd accomplished with her honey gold hair, the effect ruined by the calculating gleam of pale blue eyes.

Great, she was on the war path. Again.

Mona pasted her best hostess smile on and offered the crab a seat. "Your father was just finishing his dinner. Would you like a drink?"

Sally looked at the slightly cracked vinyl chair, wrinkled the nose her plastic surgeon gave her, and carefully dusted it off before deigning to sit. "A cup of herbal tea please, and don't forget to heat the pot before adding the water. I just hate when people get that wrong, don't you?" Her smile saccharine, she brushed Mona off like a piece of lint and turned an irritable glance on her dad. "I thought we talked about the desserts you've been eating, Daddy. You don't want me to stop these little road trips you've been taking, do you?" She looked for a place to set her suitcase of a bag down, then sighed and tucked it onto her lap. "Trace and I...," she leveraged a smug look at Mona, "... want you to stay healthy."

Yeah, so she could continue to live in daddy's mansion. Mona gave Mr. Hayward's arm a reassuring squeeze before heading to get the highness her tea. Everyone had heard the story of how Sally's father met and wooed his wife sixty-three years ago. She came from a wealthy family who didn't think the grocery store bagger was good enough for their daughter. Josiah didn't let that stop him though. He worked hard, caught the attention of the owner who gave him one promotion after another until he made manager. When the owner retired, Mr. Hayward bought the store and got the girl. A couple of years later Sally came along. His wife passed away thirty years later, leaving Sally to run the household. Much as he loved his family, Josiah wanted his daughter to marry for love, not fortune. Then Sally cast her eye on the new kid at school, and the rest, as they say, was history.

Mona tapped her toe and mumbled under her breath while waiting for the water to heat the teapot. "I need a sign for the front window, *No Skanks Allowed.*"

"Someone got up on the wrong side of the bed this morning."

She turned to see her brother taking a seat at the counter, travel mug in hand. "You weren't supposed to hear me," she muttered, some of the steam she'd been feeling escaping at the tired lines crowding Jake's forehead. She left the pot simmering and grabbed the coffee carafe. "You look like you could use this."

He gave a lopsided smile and turned his cup over. "That bad, huh?"

"Depends on if you're going for the whole dark and broody vibe or not." She filled his cup, set the pot aside, and leaned on the counter. "Want to tell me what's going on?"

He shrugged. "Big job, long drive, nothing I can't handle. Besides, that should be my line. Who twisted your panties in a knot?" He glanced around the room while taking an appreciative sip of his coffee.

She could tell the moment he saw what was bothering her. He got that look, the one that said *man, I wish Mom was here.* Well she did, too. She needed someone who listened without becoming all judgmental. Her friends thought she was an idiot for carrying a torch this long—which she totally was—and Jacob tried, but he didn't understand. Hell, neither did she.

"Sis," he started, giving her a warning look. "Don't go starting something you can't finish. Samantha needs you."

The mere mention of her daughter knocked the wind out of her sails. Jake was right. The past was the past, she didn't need to invite trouble. It usually managed to find her all by its lonesome. "How'd you get to be so smart?" she teased.

"It's in our blood," he said, tapping her forearm. "You just need to pay attention to what it's telling you."

Good advice, if only she'd listen.

"How's the new nanny?" She switched topics and waved to some regulars paying for their lunch at the till. "Jane accepting her all right?"

His gaze avoided hers. "*Jane* is, yes. But, we could have managed on our own. I'm not fond of having a stranger in the house."

Hmm, interesting. He'd been agreeable when he thought the new therapist would be someone... older. "Well, give Josie a chance. She told me a bit about her cheating fiancé—poor girl. They worked at the same hospital, did she tell you that?" She carried on without giving him a chance to answer. "I understand how she feels, Jake. She needs time to get her feet back under her. This job will be good for her, and a godsend for you. You'll see."

He gave her a skeptical look and rose. "I better get going or it'll be another late night. I just dropped by to see if Sam needed a ride to the doctors on Thursday. I remembered you mentioning she was going in for a checkup."

Mona impulsively stretched over the counter and dragged her brother in for a quick hug. They might not always agree, but they always supported each other. Family first, something Trace could never figure out.

She shook the bad thoughts away and smiled. "Thanks, but I took time off so I could be there with her. I'm hoping the doc will give her a walking cast before she kills herself on those crutches. She's such a daredevil, I don't know where she gets it from."

Jake unscrewed the lid on his thermos and waited for her to fill it with coffee. He threw five dollars on the counter and picked up his mug, grinning. "I seem to remember a reckless girl jumping off the cliff into the river and breaking her arm at about the same age Samantha is now."

Mona snorted. "That was on a dare, and you know it, Jacob Samuels." He'd promised her a ride in his new-to-him sports car if she would make the jump. There was only a few years difference between them, but when it came to school they were worlds apart. He'd been the school jock, popular and great at sports, while she'd trailed behind, still in middle school and more into the books than boys. A chance to cruise with the cool kid was too good to pass up. She'd known the moment she let go of the rope and her arm got hung up that she was in trouble. Her landing rivaled Free Willy's big escape scene, but not nearly as graceful. Jake had yelled and jumped in after her, carried her sputtering from the river amid his friends' laughter and rushed her to the hospital. Their parents grounded him for a month and took away the keys to his car. She still felt guilty about that.

"Okay, sis, see you later," Jake broke into her musings. "And remember—" he nodded toward Silly Sally and her daddy, "—treat the customers nice."

Mona nodded and waved him off. She turned back to the resting teapot, all nice and warm. She drained the water and added some ice chips from the dispenser beside the fountain pop machine. Oh yes, she planned to treat Mrs. Michaels just the way she deserved.

7

J osie smiled and waited patiently for Jane to make
her move. "Don't worry, you've got this," she
encouraged the little girl.

Jane grunted and leaned forward in her wheelchair, teeth scraping her bottom lip. "I'm stuck."

"Take your time, there's no rush."

She glanced out at the evening sky. "Daddy will be
home soon."

Josie's pulse skipped a beat. Two weeks later and
still the thought of Jacob's infrequent appearances sent
her into a tizzy. He was just so... masculine. She'd
managed to keep their interactions to a bare minimum,
but sooner or later he was going to want a report on his
daughter's progress. Hopefully, he understood her
decision to take the time to build trust with Jane before

attempting much in the way of therapy. Hence, the chess game she was currently losing.

"Your dad will have to play a game, so you can show him how good you are," she said.

Jane sighed. "He doesn't have time to play." She reached out to move a pawn, then changed her mind and slid the rook horizontally across the board, capturing an unsuspecting knight.

Josie looked at her dwindling pieces and grinned. "Just as well, it wouldn't be fair to him."

Jane giggled.

She was such a sweetheart. Jacob should be here. It should've been him teaching Jane the intricate moves of chess and taking pride in her aptitude for the game. She wouldn't be six forever, these moments were precious.

The underlying sadness in the Samuels household carried an almost physical presence. "Is your father away a lot?" she asked. She'd looked, but there were no pictures or really any feminine touches at all in the home. It was as though Jane's mom never existed. She didn't know the full situation, or if father and daughter shared treasured memories, but they were an important step in Jane's recovery. She would have to corner the dragon, so to speak, and find out what could be done to help the child.

Jane fiddled with the knight she'd captured, curls

brushing her cherub cheeks. "More now than he used to be. He says business is booming and he needs to strike while the iron's hot—whatever that means."

Or he was using his work to avoid the issues at home.

"Well, he has to have a good reputation to be that busy. You must be very proud of him." Josie moved a pawn and took a drink of the punch they'd made before the game. "Mmm, this is delicious. Did you try it yet?" As with the chess, Jane had shown a natural aptitude in the kitchen, mixing and matching juices and ginger ale into a delightful cocktail beverage. They were going to bake brownies tomorrow. Everyday tasks like these would instill confidence as well as increasing dexterity without the connotations of physical therapy. She'd found her patients performed much better under positive reinforcement and exercises that pushed conventional boundaries.

Jane reached out to the fancy snifter they'd used for the drinks, but her fingers caught the chess board and pushed it up against the glass, which was sitting too close to the edge of the table and tipped over, hitting the floor with a crash. Her mouth dropped open as the cold liquid splashed up her legs.

Josie smiled and was about to reassure the girl when Mount Samuels erupted.

"Don't move," Jacob snarled, dropping the pack

he'd walked in with and hurrying across the room to the wheelchair. "Are you hurt?" he asked his daughter, leaning over her head like a dark cloud of doom.

"N... no," she said, tears clinging to thick, dark lashes. "I'm sorry, Daddy. I didn't mean to drop the glass."

He shot Josie a cold glare. "I know that, Pumpkin. Let's get you washed up, shall we?"

He backed the wheelchair away from the table and turned towards the bedrooms. "Miss Sparks, there are towels in the kitchen. See if you can clean the mess without cutting yourself." He strode a few feet and glanced over his shoulder. "And don't go anywhere. I want to talk to you."

Josie frowned as he walked away. Accidents were bound to happen. He couldn't wrap his daughter in bubble wrap. She was bound to get hurt now and then, it was part of life.

She rescued the chess board from the river of juice dampening the wood, then side-stepped the glass to hurry into the kitchen for towels and a container for the broken pieces. Maybe they should have used Jane's plastic cups for their drinks, but Josie wasn't sorry they hadn't—even with the unhappy ending. She'd seen the little girl's eyes light up for the first time since they'd met. She didn't need to be treated with kid gloves. Most people thrived with a challenge and picking up a glass tumbler while playing a game of chess had allowed Jane to see the possibilities.

No, she wasn't sorry.

"Miss Sparks, what do you think you're doing?"

The gravelly texture of Jacob's voice rolled up her spine and caused an involuntary shiver just as she lifted jagged glass from the floor. Blood spurted. Josie gasped and dropped the offending piece into the container before reaching for a napkin to cover the wound.

"Don't yell," she snapped. Uncomfortable with him towering over her, she stood then wished she hadn't as the room swayed—or was that her?

"Whoa," he said, grasping her arm to steady her. "A nurse that can't stand the sight of blood, huh?" He urged her into a chair and left to wet a cloth in the kitchen sink.

"Therapist," she called, irritated with her temporary weakness and exasperated with him for noticing. "It's not the same thing."

He returned with a damp rag and gently took her hand. He uncovered the injury, checked for glass, then wrapped her finger. "You'll survive." He tipped her chin and gazed into her eyes. Something... heated passed between them.

Josie swallowed and held her breath.

He released her and took a step away, clearing his

throat. "My daughter has limited mobility. Please take care in the future so that you don't endanger her safety again." He waved a hand at the chess board. "And save the games for when you're off-duty, if you don't mind. I pay you to work with Jane and help her accept her lifestyle, not to throw a party."

He stomped out of the room and left her fuming. A party with a six-year-old and a glass of punch.

Go her.

Then the memory of the heat in his stormy bluegray eyes washed over her and she felt dizzy all over again.

8

Jake was still fuming three days after his run-in with the nanny. Josie Sparks rubbed him the wrong way. The instant he was anywhere near her, his senses went into overdrive. It was disconcerting, to say the least. She was a distraction he couldn't afford. The contract he'd landed with Sweet Sensations Health Spa was a big one, with the promise of future jobs down the road. He'd been commissioned to build several sleeping pods designed to blend with the landscape while encircling the main compound, like a giant grounded drone. Never mind that the concept was an eyesore on the island's pristine shoreline and he was on half the town's shit list for taking on the work. He also had Mona's wrath to contend with. The spa's owners—who were keeping their names under wraps so far—had started an aggressive ad campaign touting health and fitness over high carb meals and rich desserts, namely his sister's restaurant. So far, her clientele remained loyal, but he knew Mona felt betrayed by his decision. He planned on talking to whoever was behind the campaigns and letting them know that's not the way to make friends on a small island where everyone counted on each other for business.

He spent the morning fine-tuning the plans with his foreman. Then he drove to the Town Hall and verified the zoning clearances before stopping on the off-chance of catching the mayor.

"Hey, Trudy. You're looking particularly lovely today." He leaned on the receptionist's counter and grinned at his mother's best friend. "Is the big man available?"

She giggled, her ample bosom jiggling under a Hawaiian-styled caftan. She pushed red-rimmed glasses up her nose and peered through the bifocal lenses at an ancient computer. "You're just in time. Better make it quick, he has a meeting with Ocean and Fisheries in half an hour." She raised a pencil-thin eyebrow.

Jake nodded and tapped the counter. "Yes, ma'am. I promise not to make him late." He strode toward the closed door leading to the mayor's office. "See you at Sunday dinner."

"You bet your bottom," she chirped. "I'm making my famous strawberry cream pie for dessert."

He groaned. "You're going to make me fat if you keep feeding me like that."

She snorted. "I have to, I've tasted your cooking."

"Hey," he protested, hand on the door knob. "I thought you liked my cooking."

She shook her head and tsked. "You might be able to fool that honey-child of yours, but Mona spilled the beans. She brings meals over and all you need to do is reheat them. Good thing too, little Janey needs her strength."

Jake smiled, though his earlier humor had disappeared. "She'll be happy to see you, she knows who spoils her."

"She's easy to spoil. You have a beautiful little girl. Just like her mother."

He opened the door, anxious to escape his demons. "I better get in there. Thanks, Trudy."

The mayor looked up from the file he'd been reading as Trudy called out, "Jacob Samuels is here to see you."

Jake quirked his brow. "Got a minute?"

Trace stood and held out his hand in greeting. "For you, anytime. What brings you into town on a Thursday? I heard business has been good lately."

Jake shook his friend's hand and took a seat, appreciative of the soft leather upholstery. "Can't complain. That's why I stopped by, actually. I was hoping you could tell me who the owners of the new health spa are. I have a few questions for them but can't seem to get past their legal team."

Trace unhooked the single button holding his steel gray suit jacket fastened and resumed his chair. He closed the thick manila file, rested his hand with its heavy gold band on top and shook his head, his mouth wry. "We go back a long way, but even for you I can't reveal a private organization until they want it acknowledged."

Frustration drove Jake to the edge of his seat. "What's with the cloak and dagger attitude? Anyone could be forgiven for thinking you have a vested interest in getting this passed with as little fanfare as possible." Guilt flashed in the other man's blue eyes. Jake gripped the arms of the chair, his fingers digging furrows into the leather. "That's it, isn't it? Tell me what's going on," he demanded.

Trace shoved his chair back and strode to the floor-to-ceiling bank of windows overlooking the manicured front lawn of the Town Hall. A giant chestnut tree provided shade for the picnic table that sat beneath. A couple of teenagers were taking advantage of the space now, butts planted on the tabletop, feet resting on the bench as they tapped away on their cell phones.

"Did you realize it's been fifteen years since our graduation?" he said, hands twisting behind his back.

Jake frowned. Where was he going with this?

He joined Trace at the window and gazed at the young couple outside. He and Annie had been like that; happy as long as they were together. The soft glow of memories accompanied the lingering ache of loss. Childhood sweethearts and married at just eighteen. None of that mattered, though—they'd been crazy in love. She'd wanted to start a family right away, but it had taken eight years and countless specialist visits to make it happen. She'd named Jane after her mother, and they'd assumed the worst was behind them.

They'd assumed wrong.

"What does that have to do with the health spa?" Jacob growled, angry the past he kept carefully buried was creeping to the surface. Trace turned a sympathetic gaze on him, which didn't help.

"We used to be close, you, me, Mona and Annie. Life was simpler back then." Trace sighed. "Sally owns the land. She blames our divorce on Mona and now she's determined to ruin your family. I tried to talk her out of it, but...," he shrugged, "you know how she can be."

Sally.

As in Sally Michaels, Trace's ex-wife and master

manipulator. Thanks to that damn contract he'd signed, Jake had climbed into bed with a snake.

9

J ake rubbed the back of his neck and tried to come up with a way out of this mess. Mona would be heartbroken if she lost the restaurant. She'd put everything she had into making the place a success, so she could give her daughter chances she'd never had. "Isn't this a conflict of interest, or something?"

Trace shook his head, his mouth grim. "We were divorced *before* she snuck behind my back and had the land signed into her name. It's legal, all right." He gripped Jake's arm. "I can't tell you how sorry I am. I want you and Mona to know I'll do whatever I can to stop this insanity, but you should be prepared for the worst. With Sally's daddy getting dementia the way he did, she now controls the family reins—in other words, there's nothing standing in her way."

"We'll see about that." Jake strode toward the door, anger roiling in his gut. How had the day gone so wrong? He'd started out his morning full of excitement. This job would've been the one to cement his business on the island, allowing him more time with Jane. Now, he'd be lucky not to get embroiled in a legal battle with Sally Michaels and a war with his sister. Mona knew how important this was to him, she would fight him tooth and nail over giving it up, but they were family, he had no choice. It was funny in a sad kind of way the roads the four of them had traveled since high school. One had become a single mother and restaurant owner, another a politician, himself as a carpenter, and... Annie.

He turned and raised a hand in farewell. "I'll keep in touch. I'd appreciate if you returned the favor."

"Of course," Trace said. He hesitated, "Tell your sister I was asking about her."

Jake nodded and left the room, waving at Trudy on his way out the door. He'd never agreed with Mona's insistence on keeping Sam's paternity a secret. Trace deserved to know he had a child. Frankly, it was a mystery how she'd kept it from him this long; Samantha was the spitting image of her daddy. The longer Mona put it off, the more she jeopardized her relationship with her daughter. And speaking of daughters... He owed his girl an apology. He'd been unnecessarily harsh with her the night before and hadn't even acknowledged her accomplishment at learning the rudiments of chess. He needed to exercise better control of his emotions around Josie. She was trying, he had to give credit where it was due. Jane had seemed happier the last couple of weeks. He'd come home more than once to the sweet sound of her laughter filling the once cold house.

The one he'd bought for Annie.

She'd always dreamed of a house on a hill overlooking the sea and he'd done everything in his power to give her that dream. But it had cost him in ways he couldn't have foreseen.

When the booming economy slumped, he worked longer hours and was forced to place a second mortgage on the house. It caused numerous arguments. Annie felt abandoned and he'd been overwhelmed. He regretted it now, but it was too late. All he could do was pick up the pieces of their lives and try his damnedest to make it right.

He got into his pickup, parked in the shade of the big old chestnut tree, and glanced at the box on the floor. Good, still sleeping. His foreman had hounded him for weeks to take one of the nine puppies his Retriever had given birth to. Jake had put him off, the extra responsibility involved with training a young dog more than he wanted to handle on top of everything else, but then he'd overheard Thomas's plans to put the young pup down because he was the runt of the litter and no one wanted him. Jake couldn't let that happen, so he told the man to bring the animal to work and he'd take him. Thomas's grin had said it all—gullible much?

"What are we going to call you? Mischief maybe? Sampson? Apollo?" The pup stared up at him with timid chocolate brown eyes, then, as though he couldn't help himself, his mouth opened on a jaw-cracking yawn, revealing a row of prickly baby teeth and a pink tongue. Jacob smiled. "Energetic little critter, aren't you? Hope that black mouth means you're a smart one. Jane's going to be a pushover where you're concerned, so I'm counting on you to follow the rules, got it?" The pup tipped his head, ears cocked forward to catch every word. He gave a little whining-yelp, turned a couple of circles in the box, and curled into a furry golden ball.

"Not much of a talker, huh?"

Jacob started the truck and drove the winding road up to his home, taken as always by the grandeur of his surroundings. A robin's egg blue sky drifted into hazy clouds over the Rocky Mountains across the strait. It had been a while since he'd taken the time to just breathe in the aromatic cedar forests and the briny, bracing scent of the ocean. Even longer since he'd taken a day to enjoy it. Maybe he'd see if Jane wanted to take the puppy to the beach. Eagerness moved through his chest. They could have a picnic, spend some quality father-daughter time together. It would be like the old days, before...

He shook his head and turned up the driveway. No negative thoughts allowed. It was time he moved on. In a way, the accident had handicapped him as much as his daughter. He'd spent the past two years in a black fog of pain, so thick and impenetrable he feared he'd never escape. He was ashamed to admit he hadn't been the support Jane needed, he'd left most of the emotional side of things for his sister to handle. And now, he felt the distance between them keenly. He glanced at the pup waking from its nap and hoped his daughter would accept the peace offering as the beginning of a new chapter for them—a chance at redemption.

JOSIE MASSAGED JANE's ankles and calves. An important part of rehabilitation was not giving the muscle mass a chance to atrophy. To that end, she'd set up a regimen of easy exercises her young charge could work on twice a day without overtaxing her strength. Except, Jane had done too many repetitions and now was suffering with a Charlie horse in her right thigh. She'd only stepped out of the weight room for a moment and had left Jane safely ensconced on the floor surrounded by a mound of pillows. She'd assumed the child would be fine. Jane's determination to succeed could carry her far, she only needed to learn how to harness it. This was actually great news—it meant feeling was returning to the damaged tissue, but she didn't think Jane saw it in the same light.

"I don't want to get better if it's going to hurt this bad." Tears glistened on thick, dark lashes. "Make it go away," she cried.

"Tell me a story, honey. It'll help to get the pain off of your mind." Josie smiled encouragingly. Poor kid, she'd been through so much already. The tendons in her leg stood out like a ridge of mountains marching across her skin

"A... a story about what?" Jane hiccupped.

Josie brushed a soft brown curl behind a delicate ear. "Whatever you like. How about a campfire tale? I'll start and then you carry on, sound good?"

Jane nodded, tears forgotten.

The muscles under her fingers were loosening, and Josie sighed her relief. "Okay, here we go," she said. "The Anderson family went on a long-awaited camping trip deep into the forest. They pitched a tent, set up camp and built a fire. After a big dinner of hot dogs and s'mores, the family settled around the fire to relax before bedtime. Just then they heard a strange noise, *c...rick, c...rick.* 'What was that?' cried Momma Anderson.

"Your turn." Josie smiled at Jane's rapt look.

"I don't know what to do," the little girl said.

"Just say whatever comes to mind. There's no wrong answer here, we're making it up as we go."

Jane gave an uncertain nod. "'Umm, maybe it's an owl,' Daddy Anderson said. He got to his feet and searched the dark woods. 'Maybe we should go to bed now.'

'Aw, Daddy,' the kids cried. 'We aren't tired.'

C...rick, c...rick.

Everyone froze.

'I think it's hungry,' the youngest Anderson boy said.

'Yeah, and it likes little boys,' the eldest girl replied.

'None of that now,' Daddy warned. 'We're a team, remember?'"

Jane pointed at Josie. "Your turn," she said, her honey-brown eyes sparkling.

Josie stood and brought the wheelchair over. "Let's get you into the bath before your dad gets home. He doesn't want to hug a stinky girl," she teased. She helped Jane into the chair and leaned over to release the brake.

"But what about the Andersons?" Jane asked, twisting so she could meet Josie's gaze.

"Well..." Josie started. Just then they heard a strange sound at the front of the house.

C...*rick, crick.*

They froze, staring at each other with wide eyes.

"Th... That's not funny," Jane whispered.

She had that right.

Who was in the house and how did they get in? It didn't matter, she needed to keep Jane safe. "Shh." She put a finger to her lips and searched for a nearby weapon. The exercise room was well equipped, but the dumbbell was too heavy, the weights too dangerous—she didn't want to kill whoever it was—and nothing else was handy. The strange sounds came again. Left without options, Josie picked up the lightest weight she could find, five pounds, and hid the wheelchair behind the door.

"Stay here until I see what's going on," she murmured, waiting long enough to make sure Jane understood before edging into the hall. Her hands were slippery on the makeshift weapon and her heartbeat was so loud in her ears it was a wonder the whole house didn't hear it. How come heroines on TV handled life and death situations with assurance? She was close to hyperventilating. Then she heard the unmistakable sounds of a puppy yipping and Jacob's reassuring response and her insides turned to goo. He'd bought his daughter a pet.

"We're in the exercise room," she called, and hurried back to her charge's side, pulse fluttering wildly. "Dad's home," she told Jane and smiled at the relief shining in the little girl's eyes. No more campfire stories for a while, their nerves couldn't take it.

Jacob rounded the door a minute later, a wiggling cardboard box in his hands. He met her gaze for a warm instant before he turned his attention to his daughter. "I brought you something," he said. He kneeled beside her and lifted the blanket covering the box. A wet nose poked out the top, followed by chocolate brown eyes and cupped ears. A roly-poly puppy stared out at them, its golden fur falling in waves down its back.

"A puppy," Jane cried. "You brought me a puppy." Tears ran down her cheeks as she reached out tentative fingers to touch the dog.

Jacob looked up at Josie helplessly. "What's wrong? Why is she crying?"

Josie's heart squeezed. "Nothing is wrong. She's just incredibly happy. You did a good thing here, Daddy."

He met her gaze with gratitude and a touch of heat —or maybe she was transmitting her emotions onto him. Whatever it was, it sent her equilibrium skittering and the next thing she knew the five-pound weight she'd been holding slipped from her hand and dropped onto his arm with a dull thud.

His mouth opened in a stunned *oh*, the box tipped and out fell the pup, who scrambled onto his feet and scurried down the hall, like Josie wished she could do right about now. Jane screeched, and Jacob cradled his arm and scowled. "All in a day's work, Miss Sparks?"

She heaved a giant sigh—indeed.

10

J ake calmed his daughter as Josie rushed down the hall in hot pursuit of the runaway puppy. Not even in the house for two minutes and the mutt was causing as much disruption as the therapist. What had happened to his mundane life?

He rubbed his arm and glanced down at the weight resting against his foot, for once grateful he had to wear heavy safety boots on the job sites. The look on Josie's pretty face had been priceless. She'd apologized ten times over, and probably still would have been doing so if he hadn't sent her running after the dog.

He took Jane's hand. "What were you guys doing in the weight room?" She looked flushed. Hopefully, she wasn't coming down sick again. Since the accident her immunity wasn't at its best. He brushed wispy bangs off her forehead. "Are you feeling okay?"

Her reply was to lean away from his touch, her attention on the empty hallway. "I'm fine, Dad," she said impatiently. "Where are they? What happens if he gets out?" She turned big brown eyes on him. "The road isn't very far away, he could get hurt. Come on, let's help Josie." She backed the chair up with the controls and turned the wheels, preparing to slide past him just as Josie rounded the corner, a squiggling puppy in her arms.

"You found him," Jane called, hero worship apparent in her expression. She clapped her hands and held them out to receive the pup. Jake tensed, ready to jump to the rescue if the animal was too feisty, but he needn't have worried. Josie set the dog on her lap, then kept a calming hand on its back. Jane sat completely still, as though not sure what to do now that she held the pup.

Jake understood how she felt. He didn't know what to do with all the emotions coursing through his body, either. Annie had insisted on a pet for Jane and he'd never understood, not seeing the sense in another responsibility when his shoulders were bowing under the pressure already. But now he got it. That little ball of fluff was going to grow with his daughter and be her confidante, playmate, and guardian. The pup had a big job in front of him but going by the light in his baby girl's eyes, she thought he could handle it. Then she turned that gaze on him, and Jake was ready to slay dragons.

Josie slid him an uncertain glance, then smiled at Jane. "You can pet him, he won't bite. Have you thought of a name yet?"

The pup took matters into his own hands. With his thin tail whipping, a small pink tongue lashed out, catching cheek, nose, chin, whatever skin he could find. Jane gasped, then giggled, her fingers sinking into the soft fur.

"Daddy, look, he likes me." Her smile lit the room and warmed his heart.

Jake smiled back around the lump in his throat. "What's not to like?" he said. "Are you ready to teach this guy some manners?"

"This is the best gift ever," she chirped. "Josie will help me, won't you?"

Josie stood and brushed a wavy strand of honey-brown hair away from her face. "Well, it's been a few years since I had a puppy, but I think we can manage, yes." She leveled an unfathomable look on Jake. "Maybe your father would prefer to help?"

Jake frowned, unaccountably annoyed. He didn't need the therapist to run interference between him and his kid. If she preferred having Josie's help to his, that was fine. He didn't have time for puppy training anyway. "I have work," he muttered.

Josie glared at him over Jane's head. "Listen, I need to talk to your dad for a minute. Are you okay with your new friend, here?"

Jane nodded, her eyes shining. "Sure. I'll keep a tight hold on his collar, so he doesn't fall."

The pup had already used up his energy and fallen asleep with his head resting on the arm of the wheelchair. Jake bent and gave his daughter a kiss on the forehead. "Be right back, honey. I'm glad you like your present."

Jane hugged the pup. "I *love* him."

Josie led the way to the exercise room, Jacob followed and set the weight he'd been carrying on a bench. She glanced out to check on Jane, then closed the door and leaned against it. Her gaze made him uncomfortable, like his skin was two sizes too small.

He wandered the room, but the mirrors lining the walls bounced her image back to him every step of the way. Not that he needed any reminders, he'd spent more than one night waking up with her on his mind. It had succeeded in leaving him feeling guilty and out of sorts for the rest of the day. No wonder he'd been spending more time away from home—it was *her* fault.

Not really. He'd like to blame her, but truthfully it was his own fault if he couldn't keep his libido under control.

"How's the arm?" she asked, head tipped, wavy

hair brushing her shoulder, as she watched him making the rounds.

He glanced down, surprised by the question. "It's fine. Thanks." He met her gaze in the mirror. "You had something to say?" His tone was abrupt, but there was nothing he could do about that. She kept him off-kilter.

She straightened, her expression going from worried to wary. Good, she should be.

"Jane is over the moon about that puppy. It almost seemed as though it's her first pet."

He could tell she was bursting with questions, but he wasn't ready to give all the answers, so he just nodded.

Her face fell. "Okay, well, the thing is... I never hired on to babysit a dog." She crossed her arms and stared at the floor as though she wished a hole would open up and swallow her. "If you want the pup trained, you'll have to do it."

He stiffened, ready to... he didn't know what. Somewhere in the last few weeks she'd become indispensable to his daughter, he couldn't fire her. Then he took note of her defensive posture and her strange attitude suddenly made sense. She was doing this for Jane.

A warmth he hadn't felt in a very long time unfurled in his chest. He strode to her side and stared at her bent head. "Why didn't you tell me I was being a jerk?" That brought her head up. She stared at him with wide eyes.

"You aren't mad?" she whispered.

His lips quirked at that. "Maybe a little, but I'll get over it. Thing is, you're right. I've been so crazy at work I've neglected my child. And you." She startled, and her cheeks took on a rosy hue. He had the sudden urge to kiss her, taste that sassy mouth and see if it was half as hot as it was in his dreams.

He lowered his head and she opened her mouth. "Are you going to kiss me?" she asked, shock apparent in her expressive eyes.

He smiled. "Yes, so shush." He held her waist, more to anchor himself than to hold her in place and released the breath he hadn't even been aware of holding before touching her lips with his. The sensation was so exquisite, he had to close his eyes to hold it all in. *Good.* So damn good.

Her mouth was warm and mobile, and her hot little body practically melted in his arms. She made sweet, kittenish sounds that he felt right to the core. But when her tongue licked into his mouth the resulting explosion of sensation told him he was losing control.

He took a step back, away from her erotic moan, his body aching. The flush covering her face and neck almost drove him back to her arms, but that would be a mistake. He wasn't in a good headspace for an affair—and neither was she.

"What did you do that for?" she whispered, the back of her hand against her swollen lips.

"Hell if I know," he muttered.

She opened the door at her back, the one leading into the hall where his daughter sat waiting a few feet away. *Christ.*

"Well, don't do it again," she warned, and disappeared like a wraith.

Yeah, he'd take that as some sound advice.

11

Mona stomped up the walk and stormed in the front door of the Town Hall. "Where is he?" she growled.

Trudy looked up from her desk, startled. She glanced at the mayor's office, then stood and hurried to the front reception counter. "He's in a meeting, honey. Now calm down, you don't want to go and say something you'll regret later."

Mona laughed, though there was nothing funny about the situation, and headed toward the closed door, his lordship's name emblazoned in gold script across the wood paneling. "The only regret I have is that I didn't shoot the bastard when I had the chance."

The last words floated into the room as she opened the door and put an instant halt to the so-called secret meeting. Sally turned from her position in front of the window, a sardonic smirk on her red lips. "Fancy meeting you here," she murmured.

Trace was at the bar pouring himself a drink. He'd stiffened on her entrance and now cursed as the liquor overflowed his glass. He set the tumbler down, grabbed some napkins and crouched to sop up the mess from the sage green carpet.

His gaze met hers, a hint of appeal in his expression. "Mona, this is a surprise. I hope you'll save the shooting until after I have a drink. It's been one of those mornings." His eyes invited her to share in his humor, to remember their connection and give him a chance.

For one brief instant, she softened. Everything they'd been to each other, the memory of his touch... then Sally clapped her hands and the anger flooded back, hotter than ever.

"So sweet. Are you sure you two didn't take acting lessons? That's a theatre-worthy production if ever I've seen one." Sally lowered herself onto the leather sofa next to the window and crossed her legs as though she was awaiting the next act.

"Shut up, Sal." Trace rose and picked up his drink again. He took a healthy swallow before waving a hand to one of the club chairs in front of his desk. "Join me?" He tipped his half-empty glass in Mona's direction.

Mona shook her head but took the chair. Her knees

had been giving her problems lately and any chance to get off of them, even here, was appreciated. "We need to talk," she said, her tone abrupt. She didn't want to do this in front of his wife, but she would.

Sally sighed and rose. "Well, that's my cue. I can't stand heart-to-hearts, can you?" She wandered over to Trace, placed slim fingers with perfectly polished nails on his chest, and leaned up to buss his cheek. "See you tonight?"

Trace gave an infinitesimal nod, his gaze never straying from Mona's face. "Yeah, sure. I'll call you later."

Left with no more chaos to cause, Sally gathered up her purse and headed toward the door. "Be nice to him, Mona. I might need him later," she quipped, her smile triumphant.

Trace snorted as she closed the door. "That woman isn't happy unless she's stirring up trouble."

Which begged the question; what had he seen in her? But then, Mona could guess the answer. Sally was rich, sexy, beautiful, popular—in short, everything she wasn't.

"Why are you trying to destroy my brother's business?" She launched the first missile, well aware the best defense is a solid offence.

He looked genuinely puzzled, but then he would pretend innocence. It didn't look good in the polls if people found out how big a creep their mayor really was, and elections were just around the corner.

"I don't know what...," he started.

Pissed at the whole situation, she rose and stalked toward him, poking a blunt fingernail into his chest. "I don't want excuses, Trace. I want you to fix this. Jacob is your friend; how could you do this to him?"

He stared into her eyes and wrapped his hand around her finger, bringing it up to his lips for a kiss that made her insides quiver. She jerked her hand free and launched herself backward, her chest heaving.

"What did you do that for?" she demanded, glaring.

He smiled. *Smiled*, the jerk.

"I figured it was the quickest way to make you listen," he admitted. "Besides, I wanted to."

He was the most aggravating man on the face of the planet. "Fine, I'm listening. Explain to me why you're allowing that health spa to take up three quarters of prime waterfront real estate and when Jacob came here to talk to you about it, you put him off." She crossed her arms, hating the vulnerability she couldn't control. "Jake needs the work, but not if it's a shady corporation that's going to bleed our community dry. It'll ruin him, Trace. You've got to see that."

He stepped into her bubble—did the man have no

boundaries—and tipped her chin so he could meet her gaze. "Is that what he told you? That I put him off?"

She shrugged. Maybe not in so many words, but...

"He was protecting you, same way I'm trying to do." She startled. "Truth is, that land belongs to the Haywards. Sally's father bought it when the old Davidson place burned down, back when we were kids. Now that her dad has dementia, Sally has taken control of his business interests." He brushed his finger along her cheek. "Do you understand what I'm saying?"

She stared into eyes so blue she could happily drown in them and saw the truth he couldn't reveal. "Your wife holds my brother's future in her slimy little hands. That's it, isn't it?" She dropped her forehead to his chest, wishing she could take comfort in the strong beat of his heart. "We're doomed."

He wrapped his arms around her waist and waited, her mooring in a storm-tossed sea. "He's been through too much already, I have to do something," she muttered into his shirt.

He chuckled. "Funny, Jake said the same thing about you."

She looked up at that. "Me? What do I have to do with..." A lightbulb went off in her head. She swore. "Are you telling me this is *my* fault? Your wife is on a vendetta to ruin my brother because of *our* past? That's ridiculous."

Trace's lips quirked sadly. He released his hold on her and stepped away to pick up his drink. "Of course," he said quietly. "But that's Sally. My *ex*-wife, by the way. She gets something in her head and it's well-nigh impossible to change her mind. I have to see her tonight when I pick up Beth. I'll try to talk some sense into her, but no guarantees."

Beth. The fourteen-year-old he'd fathered a little more than a year after he'd walked out on her. Samantha's half-sister. The one she had no idea lived in the same town as she did.

Fun times.

J osie wasn't sure how she got through the next few days. She must have acted reasonably normal, because no one questioned her absent-mindedness, even when she set the puppy's food in the refrigerator instead of the pantry where it belonged. Jacob's kiss lived front and center in her thoughts, and his hard, masculine body encompassed her dreams. He was a moody, short-tempered grump who made her pulse skyrocket. How could she feel this way when only a month ago she'd been hours from marrying another man?

She added fresh-baked chocolate chip cookies to the picnic basket she'd prepared and glanced down at the pup sitting expectantly at her feet. "If you're looking for handouts, you'll just have to wait. No offence, but I don't trust your stomach in the car."

"Is it time yet?" Jane wheeled into the kitchen, her face expectant. The dog, thinking it was playtime, crouched, nose on his front paws, butt in the air and tail wagging a mile a minute. He let out a couple of excited yips, then raced around the room and jumped against Jane's shorts-clad legs. "Ow, Mischief, that hurts," she cried, then stopped in shock and stared at the red marks already fading from her skin. "It hurt," she whispered.

Josie pushed the dog out of the way and crouched at the little girl's side. "Honey, this is great. I'm so happy for you. We better tell your father, so he can get you to the specialist for a checkup."

Jane shook her head and gripped Josie's wrist. "No. Can we keep it a secret? Please, Josie? Just for a while. I want to get better and surprise Daddy by walking. *Please?*"

Her pleading eyes undid Josie. How was she supposed to say no to that? She nodded. "Okay, but if you have any pains at all, you tell me, understand?" She patted Mischief's silky head. "Guess your dad knew what he was doing, getting you a dog. Maybe we should name him Miracle instead of Mischief."

Jane giggled. "It's not Mischief, Josie. It's you. You're the miracle."

Overcome, Josie gave her an impulsive hug. "Your dad is one lucky guy," she whispered.

"What are you two conspiring about over there?" Jacob entered the house through the sliders opening onto the patio. He'd been cutting grass and must have become overheated—or lost his shirt. The sun had kissed his skin a warm golden-brown. The muscles in his arms and chest were delineated, strong from years in the construction business. A thin trail of dark hair led the way from his belly button and hid behind low-riding jeans and a growing bulge he didn't bother to hide.

Embarrassed, Josie looked up and caught amusement mixed with sinful temptation in his storm-tossed eyes. She snapped her sagging jaw shut, swung back to the overflowing hamper, and blindly moved cookies and thermoses around, her mind filled with erotic images of just how well that body could make her hum.

"Daddy, we're not co... co-spiring," Jane giggled, reminding Josie they weren't alone. "We're going on a picnic. Can you come with us?"

"Wellll," Jake murmured. "Looks like you packed enough for an army. I guess I'd better. Someone has to haul this basket around. That is, as long as Miss Sparks doesn't mind?"

His breath feathered Josie's cheek, causing her to jump. How did he move so quietly? She snapped the lid closed and skittered sideways, away from the distracting heat of his body. "Not at all, you're more than welcome. I'm sure Jane would love to spend the day with her father." She risked another glance, and yep, still no shirt. "Actually, I have some e-mails to catch up with, and you guys don't need me in the way. Go and have a nice father-daughter day. I'll get all the highlights tonight." She smiled at Jane and headed for the hallway, anxious to escape, but she hadn't counted on Jake's lightning reflexes.

He reached out and grasped her hand, stopping her in her tracks and sending Mischief on the run. "Hold on, the e-mails will wait. Doesn't a day at the beach beat one at a keyboard?" He wove their fingers together, cementing his hold on her heart as much as her hand. "Come on, Sparks. You know you want to."

"Yeah, Josie, you have to come," Jane pleaded.

There really was no contest. Stay home and mope all day or take this opportunity to make memories she could treasure later when she left the island and returned to the real world.

"Okay, but you have to help me build a sand castle," she said.

JAKE FOLLOWED Josie down the trail to the beach a short while later, his arms laden with basket and blanket and everything else the girls deemed necessary for a picnic. Jane led the way, the motor on her electric wheelchair whining as she held to a low gear for the steep decline. Mischief felt no such hindrance and tumbled down the hill and onto the sand with a puppy's exuberance and gangly legs.

The ache in his loins intensified with every step the woman in front of him took. She wore what should have been perfectly respectable linen shorts, but they served up her ass on a pretty pink platter and he was hard put not to indulge. What was the matter with him? He was acting like a randy teenager trying to score with the cheerleader. And even if he did, what then? An affair would only make for an untenable situation at home. Much as Josie tempted him, his daughter needed her more. She'd already changed immeasurably this summer. It did his heart good to see her smile and hear her laughter. He couldn't do anything to jeopardize that.

He sighed and turned his attention from the wind playing with Josie's crazy hair. "Hey, Pumpkin. Stop there and I'll carry you across the sand. Just let me get rid of this pile of stuff. You guys packed enough for Armageddon."

Josie smiled somewhat mischievously. "We needed to be prepared," she said demurely.

He risked losing the load to lean over and whisper

on his way past, "What else did they teach you in Girl Scouts, Miss Sparks?"

She sucked in a startled breath, then came back with a swift retort. "How to tie knots."

That drew him up short. He stared at her defiant face, bemused. "You'll have show me some day, they could come in right handy." He couldn't help it, he winked, then carried on down the trail whistling with her sputtering along behind him. Yep, this was going to be a fun day.

13

Josie sighed and leaned back on her elbows, curling the warm sand beneath her toes. She'd pretended a headache in order to let Jacob spend some quality time with Jane. The two of them sat near the shore, oblivious to the slap of waves hitting the beach. They were too engrossed in the intricate castle they'd built, moat included.

Her cell phone jangled, jarring her out of a peaceful doze. She sat up and pulled the phone from the pocket of her shorts. Her mother. She sighed and answered the call. "Hi, Mom. How are things in Washington?"

"Well, it's nice to know you're still alive, young lady. Your father and I have been worried sick."

Josie gazed skyward, digging for patience she didn't have. "I told you where I was going, *and* you have my number. What more do you want?" Jacob glanced up at her strident pitch. She grimaced and mouthed '*my mother*'. He gave a commiserating nod and turned back to his daughter to give her privacy.

"Josephine Alexandra, there's no need to take that tone with me. I only did what I thought was for the best. Would you rather marry a man who isn't faithful?" *Like I did?* She didn't say it aloud, but Josie heard the words anyway. Her parents shared a tumultuous relationship. She'd once asked her mom why she never divorced, and she'd looked shocked. "Why? Because we're married, that's why."

Josie rubbed her forehead. "No, of course not. I appreciate everything you did, really. It would have been nice to get a warning, however. I was humiliated, Mom. I had to get away."

"To an island in Canada?" Her mother did that weird clicking sound with her tongue against her teeth. "It should be you in Bermuda, darling. Not him. Those tickets were a gift from your father. You should have heard him when he found out where they went."

Josie stared hard at the horizon, blinking back tears for what she thought she'd had, and lost. And for her parents, too. Misguided as they were, they loved her, and she them. "Tell Daddy it's one hundred and two in Southampton. Emmett's going to burn like a lobster."

Her mother laughed. "Well then, serves him right.

And that no-good Simone, too. To think you two were best friends practically since you were in diapers. I refuse to talk to Ingrid. She should have given that girl a lesson in leaving engaged men alone."

The betrayal burned. Her mom was right. She and Simone had been like sisters. They'd shared everything from school work to parental angst, boyfriend woes, college dorm rooms, and even jobs at the same hospital. Naturally, she'd asked Simone to be her bridesmaid. She just hadn't realized they'd been sharing the same man.

Jane's cry yanked her attention down the beach. The tide had risen, and the waves were threatening the castle by the sea. Jake was bent over, his arms outstretched to lift Jane out of harm's way, but she was shaking her head, her hands frantically shoring up the sand around the moat.

Josie jumped to her feet. "Mom, I have to go. I'll call you soon, promise."

There was a slight pause, then her mother sighed. "Just don't cast us aside because you're hurt. We love you, dear."

Josie's eyes welled up again. "Love you, too. Bye, Mom." She stuck the phone into her pocket, sniffled, and hurried across the warm sand to see if she could help save a world—even if it was one made out of sand.

Jake glanced at his passengers as he drove the truck the short distance home. Jane, tuckered out by the fresh sea air, leaned against Josie's side, her head lolling back against the seat as she fought to stay awake. Josie sat in profile, her arm around his daughter, her attention fixed into the distance, expression pensive. He didn't know exactly what had transpired between her and her mother, but it had placed a decided pall on the afternoon. He'd been so caught up in his own problems, he'd forgotten she'd arrived on the island with baggage of her own.

"I'm not sure who's snoring louder, Jane or Mischief?" he murmured, bothered by her quietness.

Josie met his gaze, her eyes faraway, then she blinked and returned to him. Her lips quirked, and she nodded toward the dog sprawled on the seat next to him, his head resting on Jake's thigh. "I think you have a new admirer."

Jane sat up yawning. "Daddy has lots of admirers, Aunty Mona says so all the time."

Josie laughed. "Something you want to share?"

Jake stopped short of growling—he didn't want to scare the dog. "Aunty Mona likes to think she's a match-maker, but the only female's attention I want is yours." He reached over and affectionately rubbed his daughter's head. "No more spreading stories. That's how little girls lose TV time."

Jane grabbed her dad's hand and held it close to her heart. "Daddy, I'm your sweetheart, remember?" She batted her eyes and looked coy.

Jake sputtered, his amused gaze connecting with Josie's. "She thinks she has me wrapped around her little finger."

"Doesn't she?" Josie grinned.

His smile was bittersweet as he gazed down at his daughter's beautiful face, so reminiscent of his wife. "Yeah, she does," he answered. Warmth bloomed in his chest. They were good together, the three of them. Josie filled a void in their lives he hadn't realized existed. The past few years had been tough, but it had also brought a new closeness to his and Jane's relationship. They trusted each other. Enough to bring a woman into his life? He didn't know. She seemed to like Josie, and the nightmare of losing her mother was slowly abating... If it were up to him, he'd have to say in his heart of hearts he was ready to try again.

Instead of the guilt he expected to feel, there was more of a lightness, a sensation that Annie approved. She wouldn't want him to spend the rest of his life brooding over what might have been, just as he knew she would always be a part of him. He would keep her memory alive for his daughter, and make sure Jane never doubted how much her mother loved her.

From the moment they'd known a baby was on the way, Annie had prepared for the child they'd dreamed of having one day. She'd taken up knitting, determined to make blankets and booties and bonnets. She'd raided the library for books on healthy eating, caring for the new baby, and nursing. They'd gone shopping for a crib and a change table, mobiles and learning toys and a teddy bear named Leroy. Then came the delivery. Eight hours of excitement, nerves, worry, and finally soul-deep contentment. The first time he'd held his child in his arms, Jake cried. She was the greatest gift he'd ever received, and he'd vowed to always keep her safe.

Look how that turned out.

14

There was a luxury model car in the driveway when they returned home. Josie's sense of well-being dried up as tension invaded the cab, radiating off the big male in the driver's seat.

"Whose car is that, Daddy?" Jane lifted her chin, trying to get a glimpse of their unknown guest through the front windshield.

Jacob's arm stretched out like a bar across her chest as he hit the brakes bringing the truck to a grinding halt. "It's business. Josie, take her inside, please."

The grim tone of his voice warned her whatever this was, it wasn't a pleasure call. "Okay, Miss Muffet, let's get you in the house and cleaned up before the dirt fairies carry you away."

Jane giggled. "That's silly, there's no *dirt* fairies."

"Are you willing to take a chance on that?" Josie

tickled her belly and hopped out of the truck at the same time a leggy blonde unfolded herself from the driver's seat of the car. A sleeveless burgundy tank top highlighted golden arms covered in bejeweled bangles. White jeans with strategic rips in the knees covered slim hips and narrowed down to black suede lace-up boots with three-inch heels. They locked eyes and Josie's instinct was to get back in the truck and demand Jacob get them out of there. Even at this distance she shivered under the other woman's ice pick gaze stabbing her in the chest.

"Friend of yours?" she murmured.

Jake grimaced. "A client. And the ex-wife of a buddy, so be nice." He opened his door and strode around back to unload Jane's wheelchair, then joined them on the passenger side. "Ready?" he asked, reaching into the truck to lift his daughter into his arms.

Josie's pulse had leaped at his approach, and now her breath stuck in her throat. The man had some serious biceps, and he smelled of the sea—heady stuff.

"What about Mischief? He's going to fall," Jane cried. She craned her head over her dad's shoulder as he lowered her into the chair. The dog stood on the edge of the seat, tail wagging so hard he almost overbalanced. Josie hurried forward and grabbed his collar, holding him in place.

"Hang on, you little rascal." She rubbed the silky ears and smiled when the pup licked her palm.

"Set him down. He'll follow you into the house," Jacob said.

Blondie fisted her hands on her hips and pursed pink lips. "Jake, your nanny can surely handle your ki... child. We need to talk, and I don't have much time."

Jacob frowned, his brows angry slashes over stormy gray eyes. "I'll be there in a moment, Sally. Give it a rest."

Josie set the dog on the driveway and rose in time to catch an eyeroll from the other woman. She brushed her hands down her thighs and forced a smile. "Let's get out of their way, Jane. If you hurry to get cleaned up, I'll make you an ice cream float. How does that sound?"

Jane clapped her hands. "Yay, ice cream." She turned to her father. "Are you coming, Daddy?"

He leaned over and kissed her forehead. "Soon, peanut. Save me some, okay?"

The ice cream was the incentive Jane needed. She motored up the drive, barely glancing at the stranger as she headed for the front door. Mischief chased the wheelchair's tires, nipping at the rubber as though he was herding a stray sheep.

Josie placed hesitant fingers on the warm skin of Jacob's forearm, and met his surprised gaze. "Are you all right out here?" she asked, and then wished she'd bitten her tongue when he grinned.

"Are you offering protection, Miss Sparks?"

The intimate rumble of his voice hinted at an entirely different cover than the one she'd been envisioning.

"No!" she gasped. "I mean... if you need help, I'm here."

He smirked. "I'll take you up on that... later."

Her cheeks burned. Who knew innocent words could take on dirty meanings just by a raised eyebrow?

She trailed after Jane and the puppy, her mind filled with images of her and Jake in bed. He would be a considerate lover, it was there in his nurturing personality. In the way he'd helped her when she arrived, even though he didn't want her in his home. In the kindness he'd shown by giving a defenceless pup a home and his daughter all the love a father could show. She had goosebumps just thinking about his big hands covering her breasts, his lips on hers, body to body, heart to heart.

"He's not available, you know."

The blonde's patronizing voice snapped the daydream in half. Josie blinked and looked into the other woman's amused gaze. "Excuse me?"

She nodded toward Jake unloading the rest of the

picnic gear from the truck. "Jacob's... interests, shall we say, lie in another direction."

Stunned, Josie hesitated on her way to the house. "Are you suggesting you and he are... are..."

"Having sex, dear. And that's between me and him. I recognized the moon-eyes and wanted to save you any misery down the road." Sally smiled sympathetically. "Jake's had women chasing him since grade school, don't feel bad." She slid a pair of dark sunglasses onto the bridge of her nose. "We have a long history, he and I. It's complicated. I don't expect you to understand."

Josie stiffened.

"I have the resources to make Jake an extremely wealthy man, but lately his attention has been, shall we say, less than attentive." She smiled as Jacob strode toward them. "You don't want to ruin his chances, do you?"

Josie's heart plummeted. She hadn't realized until it was snatched away how much she'd come to care for this family. For Jake.

He gazed at them quizzically. "You ladies getting along?"

Sally's laugh tinkled like chips of ice running down Josie's back. "Of course, silly. Your nanny seems charming."

"She's not *my* nan...," Jacob started.

"Therapist actually," Josie interjected. "And I better get back to work." Her gaze skimmed the two beautiful people standing side-by-side. "It was nice to meet you," *not*, she said to Sally. She turned to Jacob. "Jane had fun today, thank you." She ended it there before she said something she'd regret, like "why did you kiss me like there was no tomorrow when you're obviously involved with someone else?" She had the worst taste in men. What was it, did she have a stamp on her forehead that said, *Cheat on me, I like it*, or what? Frustrated as much with herself as him, Josie followed the child and dog into the house.

JAKE STARED after Josie's disappearing back and wondered what he'd missed. He'd mistakenly thought she'd enjoyed herself today as much as he and Jane. It was a long time since he'd taken time from his work to relax. It felt good. And having a beautiful woman to share it with hadn't hurt either. Josie ignited a maelstrom of feelings inside him. Affection, frustration, lust, confusion, you name it, he lived it.

"What did you say to her?" he demanded, glaring at Sally. The vibrant young woman he and Trace had fought over in high school was long gone. In her place was a bitter shell. He tried to have empathy, after all, she had faced a nasty divorce and the diagnosis of her father's dementia all in the same year. That would be enough to throw the strongest person for a loop, but she was going too far in her bid to destroy his sister. Jake wouldn't stand for it.

Sally shrugged one elegant shoulder. "We were just getting acquainted. She seems... cute." The sarcasm practically dripped from her lips.

"Leave her alone, Sal. She's not in your league."

That made her laugh. "You can say that again," she murmured. He wheeled to go into the house and she grasped his arm. "Look, I'm sorry. I really did need to talk. Give me a minute?"

He gazed at the pink nails digging into his forearm until she let go. "I know what you're up to, Sally. Mona is no danger to you. She's worked hard to make her business a success, don't ruin it."

"Is that a threat?" she said, chin in the air. "I don't need to prove myself to you or anyone else. There are enough customers for both of us, and besides, a little competition is healthy, isn't it? Well, unless you're serving heart attacks on a plate, but that's not my problem." She lifted a placating hand. "I'm not here to argue. I just wanted to let you know Daddy gave me full power of attorney, so we can move forward with the rest of my plans for the spa. Isn't that exciting?"

Jake frowned. "I'm not sure you're hearing me. I'm

not going to build your spa if you intend to ruin my sister. Find another contractor."

Sally's smile froze. She opened her car door and used it as a buffer between them. "We signed a deal, Jake. Don't make me take you to court. You'll lose." She slid into her seat and fired up the engine with a throaty roar. "It was nice seeing you, maybe we can go out sometime."

She didn't wait for his answer, instead she threw the car into gear and whipped around in his drive just as Mischief raced out of the house, right into the path of the oncoming tires.

15

Josie heard the squeal of brakes and ran for the door, her heart thundering. *Jake. Oh, God, Jake. Don't let him be hurt, please don't let him be hurt.*

"What happened? Was that lady mad at Daddy?" Jane called from behind her, the whir of her wheelchair echoing in the quiet house.

"I don't know. Stay here." She pushed the partially open door and stepped into the sun, squinting against the light. At first, she couldn't see anything beyond Sally's car idling diagonally on the road, the driver's door hanging open. Then she caught sight of Jacob's dark hair over the hood with Sally crouched near the front bumper and a cry rose from the depths of her soul.

"Jake!" His head jerked up and he met her

concerned gaze. She hurried forward, her relief short-lived when she rounded the front of the car and saw Mischief lying on his side, little whining cries letting her know he'd been hit. "Oh, no," she sobbed, her hand covering her mouth. "Is it bad? I'm so sorry. I must not have closed the door when I went into the house. Jane will be devastated." Helpless tears rolled down her cheeks. She hated to see an animal in distress.

Sally stood and pointed an accusing finger at Josie. "I knew you were trouble," she sneered. "This is your fault."

Jacob glared. "This isn't the time. Someone call for help."

Sally shot her a triumphant glance beneath her lashes and turned toward her car. "I'll call, Jake. My phone is right here."

Josie wrung her hands, feeling about two feet tall. Why hadn't she taken the time to properly latch the door? She wasn't fit to care for a child. What if it had been Jane who'd been hurt? Jane lying helpless with her father looking on? Josie would never be able to live with herself.

"Jake...," she whispered, lost for words. She looked into Mischief's sad brown eyes and her throat closed.

"The car barely clipped him. He's going to be fine. Aren't you, boy?" Jacob ran a gentle hand down the dog's side and his tail thumped the ground.

"I don't know what to say," she said, bending to touch her favorite spot, the pup's soft ears. "That was so careless of me. When I think what could have..."

Jake shook his head. "Don't. We'll talk about this later. Right now, I have to worry about getting this guy better."

Josie sniffled and nodded. She couldn't blame him if he let her go after this episode. "Sure, I understand." She surreptitiously wiped the tears away and stood to check if Sally had gotten through to animal rescue. She noticed Jane coming out of the house, glanced down at Jake and the dog and hurried to intercept the child.

"Jane, I told you to stay in the house," she scolded.

Jane's expression became mulish. "I want my daddy," she shouted.

Josie hesitated, surprised by the usually sunny-natured girl's transformation. Obviously, she'd picked up on the stress and needed reassurance. First, she needed to get her away from the accident.

"C'mon, kiddo. Your dad is busy right now, he'll be in soon. Let's go make him a cold drink, okay?" She moved to turn the wheelchair around but cried out when Jane hit the forward button and the wheel ran over the end of her toes. *Ow, that hurt!*

"Jane, stop," she called, limping after the runaway, desperate to reach her before she got too close.

Mischief lifted his head, hearing his mistress's

motorized chair, and tried to rise, dragging himself toward the little girl. Jake lunged after the dog at the same time Jane saw her pet's distress and cried out, stopping her chair's momentum. Jake caught the pup and eased it back into a prone position, murmuring soothing words while gazing at Jane, misery apparent in his eyes.

"I'm so sorry, poppet," he started, then stopped, his eyes widening in shock when she levered herself out of the chair and took a couple of ungainly steps before Josie could reach her side and wrap an arm around her waist, holding her up. "Jane?" he croaked. "For the love of God, Jane, you're walking."

"I... I wanted to surprise you," the little girl whimpered. "Daddy, what's the matter with Mischief?" She considered the awkwardly parked car and Sally who'd moved next to Jacob and made the connection. "You hit my doggie!"

Sally actually had the grace to look dismayed. "It was an accident. Your dog came out of nowhere. I tried to stop. Tell her Jake, you know I tried. It's your nanny's fault. She left the damn door open."

Jane lifted tear-drenched eyes to Josie. "How could you?" she whispered. "I thought you were my friend."

"Jane," her father warned.

Josie's heart was surely shattering. She could actually feel great shards breaking off and stabbing her in the chest. She'd made the mistake of opening herself up to the hope of a second chance at love with this amazing family, but, just like with her fiancé, once again she wasn't enough.

"Help will be here soon. Try not to worry, okay?" She lowered Jane onto the pavement near Mischief's head and stepped back as child and dog comforted each other with hugs and cries.

"I have to go," she murmured, meeting Jake's probing gaze. There was so much she wanted to say, but not here, not now. "I really am sorry."

Ignoring Sally's inelegant snort, she turned and hurried toward the house and the safety of her room. At least for the moment. There was little doubt Jake would have her on the next plane leaving the island. She gasped on another sob. Even if he did forgive her for Mischief's accident—please, don't let it be serious— he'd never forgive her for withholding his daughter's progress. She'd seen the stunned, betrayed look on his face.

It was over.

16

Time dragged while they waited for the vet to arrive and assess the dog. Jake was ready to pull his hair out. Jane was inconsolable, positive her poor pooch was going to "die and go to Heaven with Mommy." He did what he could to reassure her, but truthfully, he just didn't know. It looked bad. Every time the pup tried to scramble to his feet his back legs wouldn't hold him, and he'd fall. It was hard to watch. Harder still to keep him from moving. He sensed his mistress's distress and wanted to comfort her.

After Josie ran into the house Sally had finally taken a hint and driven away. She'd insisted he send all the veterinary expenses to her accountant, so maybe there was hope for her yet. He knew it was an accident, but if she hadn't taken off in a tiff it never would have happened. He'd flat out told her if she didn't back off on her vendetta against Mona he would quit, and he didn't give a damn if she took him to court. Thankfully, she didn't call him on his bluff, but she sure as hell let him know he'd pay if he was late on his deadline. He'd worry about that later, right now he needed to calm his daughter down before she made herself sick.

"Jane, honey, quit that caterwauling now. You're scaring your puppy."

Jane glanced up from between her arms. Her eyes were red, her nose was running, and her hair a mess. Jake couldn't love her more. She reminded him of her mother with her soft heart and stubborn personality. He'd often teased Annie about her thin skin when it came to animals. She was always bringing rescue critters home from the animal shelter where she'd worked.

"Pretty soon there won't be any left to adopt," he'd teased.

She'd laughed. "We have the room. I can't stand to see them in those cages."

And so they'd collected a menagerie; cats, dogs, parakeets and cockatiels. And then Jane came, and their world was full. After Annie's death, he hadn't been able to stomach the animals, they reminded him too much of his wife. He could barely stand to be around his daughter —God, forgive him—and the neighbors had stepped in and taken them away while Mona cared for Jane.

He'd figured he would spend the rest of his life alone, and probably would have to, if not for a wavy haired, green-eyed nymph who woke him up to the possibility of second chances.

"Daddy, did I make Josie cry?"

Jane's woebegone expression lightened his heart. His baby was growing up, taking responsibility for her actions. "I'm sure she knows you didn't mean it, poppet. You have to remember words hurt, but they can also heal. I bet a sincere apology will go a long way. As soon as the doctor fixes Mischief, we'll come home and cook a nice dinner for Josie, so she knows we like her, okay?"

Jane leaned over and nuzzled her pup's head. "I love her as much as I love Mischief." She sat up and stared into his eyes. "Can Josie stay here forever? I don't want her to leave."

Jake met his daughter's gaze, and a shock ran through his body. He didn't want Josie to leave, either. Without him realizing it, she'd filled all the empty nooks in his life with her contagious laughter, sweet smiles, and generosity. He wasn't sure what their relationship might lead to, but he damn sure knew he wanted the chance to find out.

He started to rise, then realized he couldn't leave Jane out here on her own with an injured dog. He glanced down the driveway for the hundredth time, where was that vet? And speaking of rising...

"When were you going to tell me you could walk, young lady?" He'd gone through a crazy cocktail of emotions seeing her take those first steps like that. Joy, hurt, elation, and even injured pride because it wasn't him who'd helped her on the path to healing. But mostly, he was grateful. So very grateful.

Jane grinned, obviously proud of her accomplishment. "Isn't it the greatest? I made Josie promise to wait just until I could walk to you. We've been practicing every day. I wanted it to be a big surprise."

"Oh, it was," he answered wryly. "I almost fainted."

That caused a riot of giggles, which in turn excited the puppy. Even though Jake held him down, he tried to jump up and dance around them like he normally would but fell over when his back legs refused to cooperate. The laughter died, and Jane gazed worriedly from her dog to him.

"Did Mischief lose his legs b'cause I got mine back? He can have them, I'm used to not walking. Really."

Jake swallowed hard around the ball in his throat. "I'm pretty sure Mischief wants you to keep your legs, sweetheart. I think I hear the vet coming now. Let's wait and see what he has to say, okay?"

Sure enough, a utility van rounded the corner at

the end of the road and roared up the driveway. It slowed as it neared them, and a jovial, middle-aged man hopped out of the cab.

"Well, what have we got here?" he said, kneeling next to the pup with a smile for Jane. "Did your dog have an accident?"

Jane stared at him wide-eyed. "Uh, huh. Daddy's boss ran over him with her car and now he can't walk. Just like me," she added.

The man looked at Jake, recognition flashing in his faded blue gaze. "Aren't you the Samuels kid? I went to school with your father."

The joy with small towns, everyone knows your history.

"Yep, that's me." Jake watched as the doctor ran experienced hands along the dog's flank. "Do you think it's serious?"

The doc shook his head. "Nah, likely a pinched nerve. I don't feel any breaks, but we better get him in for x-rays just to be certain." He turned to Jane. "Ever ride in the back of a cube van, missy?"

Jane's eyes widened. "No, sir."

"Well," he said, glancing at Jake, "if your daddy thinks it's all right, I could use an assistant with this here patient until we get him to the hospital. You interested?"

Jane looked apprehensive, before leaning over to hug Mischief. "Oh yes, please!"

Jake nodded and rose to retrieve Jane's wheelchair for the trip. He hesitated by the front door. Should he run in and let Josie know where they'd gone?

"Daddy, hurry up," Jane called.

Sighing, he turned and pushed the wheelchair to his daughter's side.

17

Josie stayed hidden behind the gauzy curtains that covered the sidelight next to the door until the van carried Jacob and Jane out of sight. She'd already decided to stop cowering inside and was in the act of changing from beach sandals to sturdier shoes for the trip to the veterinary clinic when she overheard the voices. Not wanting to interrupt, she'd waited at the window while Jake spoke to the doctor examining Mischief. Then, he'd risen and strode toward the door and she'd thought he was coming to apologize. Her pulse leapfrogged in her chest. Instead, he'd taken the wheelchair and loaded Jane into the waiting van while the doctor carried Mischief, and they'd driven away.

Served her right.

Why should she assume he would forgive her that easily? She'd allowed herself to become invested in this family against her better judgement, but the time had come to leave. She knew what it felt like to be betrayed by someone. Jake would never forgive her for keeping quiet about Jane's condition.

And he shouldn't.

She'd messed up, end of story. Not quite the one she'd envisioned while daydreaming on the beach, but then, what were the chances he'd fall for someone like her anyway?

She hurried past the great room where the family had met in the evenings, sometimes to talk, many times to read or watch movies together. Simple times that would have to provide memories for an empty future. The pictures now sitting on the baby grand piano of Jacob and Jane, she bypassed altogether. If she looked at them she'd never have the courage to make the break. And yet, it was easier this way than waiting to be told to leave.

Maybe her mother *was* right. Maybe she did sabotage relationships rather than ending up like they had, living a cold war until even that was too much, and they'd divorced. All Josie remembered was needing love and support from the two people she should have been able to count on the most, and instead finding herself in the middle of a power struggle where she was the pawn. She'd vowed then to never allow her own children to go through that kind of trauma, yet here she was, thirty years old and on the brink of another disastrous romance.

Urgency attached wings to her steps. She just wanted to go home and lick her wounds. Try to decide where to go from here. She could look for other private sector jobs—though they didn't appeal after working for Jacob—or she could go back to the hospital and act as though everything was fine, even though it was a lie. She didn't care so much about Emmett anymore, but if she ran into Simone she might feel the urge to add Mentos to her Diet Coke.

As she packed her suitcases, Josie called the float plane company, praying they had a seat available.

"Well, hello little lady," the pilot Troy answered on the third ring. "You're leaving our fair island already? Summer's only half over."

Josie held the phone between her shoulder and her ear as she folded the shorts she'd worn to the beach, remembering Jacob's appreciative gaze. "I... have to get back to work," she said. It was the truth, after all. She had savings, but it wouldn't last long without an income, and besides, she needed to stay busy, so she didn't have time to think.

"Can you be here within the hour?" he asked, then held the phone away to shout, "Hold your horses, I'm on the way." He came back online, "Sorry about that, dang tourists. Anyhow, I'm on a tight schedule, so if you can get down here I'll save you a spot, otherwise it'll have to be next week."

Oh, no, no, no. There was no way she could stay here and act as though everything was normal for another week. "I'll be there," she muttered, and hung up before she changed her mind.

JAKE SIGNED the papers at the front counter of the veterinarian's office and sighed his relief. Mischief had undergone a battery of blood tests, x-rays, and a CT scan and sailed through all with positive results. The doctor was sure he'd suffered a pinched nerve and recommended a week's dosage of muscle relaxants and pain killers to ease the stressed area. He'd been anesthetized for the scan and would spend the night at the clinic.

He glanced down at Jane quietly waiting in her chair to go home. Poor kid, she looked wiped. They'd sat in the waiting room for what felt like hours before the doctor came out to give them his results.

"Tired, kiddo?"

She looked up at him with teary eyes. "Do we have to leave Mischief here, Daddy? He's going to be so scared when he wakes up without us."

His heart flopped. He crouched beside her and

took her hand. "You want Mischief to get better, right?"

She nodded and squeezed his fingers. "I'm scared."

Oh, man. He brushed her bangs off her forehead and touched the end of her nose with his forefinger. "None of that now. We have to think positive. When we get home, you can send a prayer up to Heaven for him to get better, okay?"

She lunged forward and wrapped her arms around his neck. "You're the best daddy ever."

He breathed in her sweet-little-girl scent and counted his blessings. He was the lucky one. "We're a good team, you and I."

The receptionist cleared her throat and Jake glanced over to see her dabbing her eyes with a tissue.

"You and your daughter are an inspiration," she gushed. "If you only knew how many times we've had to deal with impatient parents and bratty children..."

Jake smiled over Jane's head. "This one has her moments," he teased.

She jerked her head up and almost clipped his chin. "Daddy, that's not what you say. You always tell me I must have floated down from Heaven, b'cause I'm an angel."

He chuckled and rose to accept the paperwork. "When will we be able to pick the dog up?"

The receptionist clicked a few keys on the

computer and jotted the date and time on a card. "Doctor Roy would like to keep an eye on him for a day or two, make sure the anesthetic wears off and there are no other complications. I'm sure you can take him home Monday or Tuesday afternoon. If there are any changes we'll give you a call, and of course you're welcome to visit during business hours. Though I have to warn you, it usually upsets the animals more than if you wait until they can go home."

Not ideal, but if it gave Jane back her dog the wait would be worth the worry.

"Thank you... Annette." He read her nametag and nodded toward Jane. "It's going to be a long weekend for someone I know."

Annette blushed, her cheeks turning a becoming pink. "I wish there was more I could do." She smiled at Jane. "Don't worry, Dr. Roy will make sure your pup has the very best of care."

Jane nodded and played with the laces on the bottom of her shirt.

Jake thanked the lady again and wheeled them out into the late afternoon sunshine. "Who'd like an ice cream cone?" he asked. He was anxious to get back home, so he could talk to Josie, but Jane needed some cheering up after this ordeal. Plus, he could ask Mona to give them a lift, rather than calling a cab. Win-win.

Jane's expressive eyes lit up. "Me, me!" She

bounced up and down. "Can I have chocolate dipped, Daddy? Are we going to Aunty Mona's? Is Sam there today?"

Jane adored her older cousin, Samantha, with good cause. For a young teenager, Sam had a surprisingly good head on her shoulders and always had time for Jane's incessant questions.

He started to push his daughter down the sidewalk, enjoying the light breeze and tree-covered street. "Yes, you can have chocolate-dipped, that sounds good. I thought we'd ask Aunty for a ride home after, and no, I don't know if Samantha is there. She should be getting rid of her cast soon, shouldn't she?"

Jane nodded knowledgeably. "She had it removed last week. She says her leg looks gross now, all white and scaly." She giggled.

Wow, Jake couldn't believe how fast the time had flown. He missed so much with the heavy hours he kept. He looked down at his daughter's curly hair. Time to make some changes. If he kept going this way, his girl would be a woman before he knew it.

His phone jangled in his pocket. He dug it out, surprised to see Troy's name on the screen. "Jake here," he answered. "How's it going, bud? Did I have a shipment come in that I forgot about?"

"You need to get down here, quick. She's... I can't

hold her here for long," Troy whispered, his voice cutting in and out in Jake's ear.

Jake held the phone away and stared at the screen. What was the old coot talking about? He couldn't hold who...?

Shit, Josie.

"Troy, Troy please. Do what you have to do, just don't move. I'm on the way." He snapped the phone closed and cursed. Why was she leaving without a good-bye? What the hell was going on?

"Daddy, you sweared." Jane's eyes grew big.

Jake's gaze swiveled from Jane in her wheelchair to the suddenly daunting road down to the wharf. He crouched by Jane's side, his hand on her knee. "Listen, sweetheart. We need to run like the wind. Josie is getting on an airplane right this minute, and if we don't hurry we won't get there in time to tell her we want her to stay. You *do* want her to stay, right?" He squeezed his daughter's knee and held his breath. What would he do if she said no?

She nodded so hard her chair shook. "She can't leave, we love her."

Jake sighed his relief and moved around to grip the arms of the wheelchair. Jane was right, they did love Josie. Now he just had to figure out a way to prove it. "Hang on, this is going to be a bumpy ride."

18

J osie paid the cabbie and thanked him for the ride while trying to ignore the curious glances he gave her in the rear-view mirror. She'd lived in a big city her whole life and still wasn't used to how fast news travelled in Sweetheart Cove.

"If you don't mind my saying, are you sure this is what you want to do?" he asked, his kindly eyes warm as he removed her bags from the trunk and closed the lid. "Folks around here have been mentioning how much better young Jane is doing, and Jacob, too. You've been a breath of fresh air to that family—one they sorely needed."

She dug in her purse and offered a substantial tip, touched by the genuine caring this stranger had shown for the Samuels family. He tried to hand it back and she shook her head, near tears. "No, you keep it. I wish... I wish things were different, but Jane will be fine without me. She's a strong little girl."

The cabbie nodded. "She comes from good stock," he agreed. "What about Jacob though? Will he be fine if you leave?"

Troy exited the harbor plane office and strode across the tarmac, coffee mug in hand. "You made it, I see. Was just about to give up on ya." He glanced up the road behind them as though looking for someone, then grinned at the cab driver. "Still scaring innocent people out of their hard-earned money, are ya, Fred?"

Josie sucked in a startled breath, but Fred just chortled. "Says the guy who should have retired that rust bucket he flies in ten years ago." He glanced sheepishly at Josie. "Just joshin', ma'am. The Betsy Boop is a classic, she'll run forever." He jabbed Troy's arm. "Even with this old coot at the controls."

"Watch who you're calling old, buddy. Don't forget we went to the same school, and I did more than go through the front door and out the back." Troy laughed.

Fred scowled.

Josie felt the need to defend her new-found friend. "We all make mistakes."

They both turned to her and raised an eyebrow.

"What?" she said. "I know what it's like to be judged unfairly. That's all I'm saying." She looked pointedly at the three impatient people waiting on the dock near Troy's plane, two businessmen in three-piece suits and a young woman in a pretty summer dress and floppy straw hat like the one Josie was wearing to conceal her eyes. "Shouldn't we be going?"

Troy glanced nervously up the street again and took hold of the handle of her bag. "Yeah, sure. Better get underway. See you next week, Fred. Don't do anything I wouldn't do."

"What does that leave?" Fred grumbled good-naturedly. "Keep your wings in the air, buddy." He opened his car door and rattled the keys in his pocket. "Look, ma'am, if you change your mind give me a call. I'll gladly pick you up free of charge and take you home."

Home.

Josie nodded, too overcome to comment. Was she making a mistake? Emmett had bruised her heart when he'd broken their engagement, but it wouldn't compare to the gut-wrenching pain she'd feel if Jake wasn't serious about her.

Impulsively, she hugged the older man. "Thank you," she whispered, afraid it was too late. She'd already left her heart behind.

JAKE RAN the last two blocks to Main Street which fronted the wharf. The closer he got, the more he feared he was too late and Josie was gone. It didn't matter. If he had to hop a plane and go after her, then by God, that's what he'd do.

At the very least, he needed to see her face-to-face and make it clear he didn't blame her for keeping Jane's secret, or for Mischief's accident. How could he fault her for giving his daughter back to him? They'd drifted apart in the last two years—his fault, all of it. Josie, with her compassion and kindness, had seeped into their hearts and woken him up to what he'd been missing.

Her smile warmed his heart and her kisses stirred an aching within him that he'd never thought to feel again. Her body was a sweet temptation he couldn't resist. He dreamed of waking up to her silky hair brushing his bare skin, the touch of her mouth, the feel of a fast-beating heart—hers, his—the look in her beautiful green eyes after a night of passion. The whispered endearments and lazy morning-afters.

Hell, yeah. He wanted all that and more.

"Can you see her? Is she gone?"

The fearful tone in Jane's voice had him putting on a last burst of speed and they cleared the hill just in time to see Josie walking down to the dock with Troy.

"Faster, Daddy. Faster." Jane shrieked. "Josie, wait. Josie, it's us. Don't go!"

Josie glanced over her shoulder and skidded to a stop. Her hand went to her brow to get a better look at who the two idiots were yelling their fool heads off. She hesitated, then hurried toward Troy waiting by the open door.

Jacob slowed, his heart surging forward as though to reach out and tug her back to them. But, he couldn't force her. It had to be her decision. Jane began to sob. Hell, his own eyes were misty. He reached down and squeezed her shoulder, but remained where he was, frozen in place as his future prepared to ride away into the proverbial sunset.

Suddenly she turned, dropped her purse, threw her hat on the ground, hiked up her skirt, and sprinted up the hill towards them!

Jake blinked, hardly daring to believe what he was seeing while Jane's shouts of joy rang in his ears. He applied the brake for the wheelchair, half afraid she would bounce it right out of his white-knuckled grip.

"Jane, honey, settle down. We have to wait and see what she says. She might only be coming to say good-bye." He closed his eyes and lifted his head to Heaven. *Please, let her stay. Please.*

By the time she reached them, Josie's chest was heaving, and her cheeks were flushed. She looked so beautiful it hurt to think he might lose her.

"Hi," she breathed.

"Are you leaving us?" Trust Jane to lay it on the line.

"Sorry," he said. "She... *we*, don't want you to go." God, he was no better than his daughter. What happened to all his negotiation tactics that he used daily at work? Except, this was so much more important than his job. Josie was the key to his and Jane's happiness. He needed her to understand that.

He moved from behind the chair and took her hands. She gripped him back, causing a surge of hope. He looked into her eyes and everything clicked into place, the future he wanted them to have became crystal clear. She wasn't his for now, she was his forever.

"Josie, I know I'm not the most understanding of men, but I promise to always tell you the truth. If you stay, I will do my level best to make sure you never regret it. You've taught me to live again. You've given the bond of friendship and affection to my daughter, and you've made us into a family. Please, Josie, give us a chance. Give *me* a chance." His stomach did cartwheels as he tried to read what she was thinking. And then, he saw the glow of happiness lighting her gorgeous green eyes and he knew they were going to be all right.

She gave a little chirping cry and threw herself into his arms. "I'm such an idiot," she whispered against his neck, sending delicious shivers down his back. "I almost gave up the best thing that ever happened to me." She leaned back and met his gaze, her lips trembling. "I love you."

Jane clapped as elation exploded in his chest. Laughing, he picked Josie off her feet and twirled her around and around. "God, woman, you gave me a scare." He set her down and gently kissed her lips. "Let's go home."

"Wait. Can we go for ice cream now, you promised?" Jane wheedled, an innocent expression on her face.

Jacob grinned. "You heard her, the boss has spoken."

They all looked at each other and burst out laughing.

AFTERWORD

Reviews are the lifeblood of any successful author. Without you, we can't be heard.

If you enjoy the story, please consider sharing on your favorite social media sites, as well as GoodReads and from wherever you've bought the book.

Thank you,
Jacquie Biggar
Jacqbiggar.com

ABOUT THE AUTHOR

JACQUIE BIGGAR is a USA Today bestselling author of Romantic Suspense who loves to write about tough, alpha males and strong, contemporary women willing to show their men that true power comes from love.

She is the author of the popular Wounded Hearts series and has just started a new series in paranormal suspense, Mended Souls.

She has been blessed with a long, happy marriage and enjoys writing romance novels that end with happily-ever-afters.

Jacquie lives in paradise along the west coast of Canada with her family and loves reading, writing, and flower gardening. She swears she can't function without coffee, preferably at the beach with her sweetheart. :)

Sign up now to keep up with Jacquie's new releases, excerpts, giveaways, and more:

Newsletter

jacqbiggar.com
jbiggar@jacqbiggar.com

facebook.com/jacqbiggar

twitter.com/jacqbiggar

instagram.com/jacqbiggar

amazon.com/author/jacquiebiggar

bookbub.com/authors/jacquie-biggar

goodreads.com/JacquieBiggar

pinterest.com/jacqbiggar

My Girl

Married to The Texan- Box set

BLUE HAVEN

Sweetheart Cove

Sunset Beach

MEN OF WARHAWKS

Skating on Thin Ice

The Player

SINGLE TITLES

Silver Bells

The Lady Said No

My Baby Wrote Me A Letter

Tempted by Mr. Wrong

Valentine: A Hearts and Kisses Romance

Mistletoe Inn

The Sister Pact

Perfectly Imperfect